T3-ANT-728

The Adventures of
Don Quixote

by

Miguel de Cervantes

CORE CLASSICS

SERIES EDITOR MICHAEL J. MARSHALL

ABRIDGED BY MICHAEL J. MARSHALL

FROM THE TRANSLATION OF DOMINICK DALY

LIBRARY OF CONGRESS CATALOG CARD NUMBER: 98-73795

ISBN 1-890517-10-0 TRADE PAPERBACK

ISBN 978-1-890517-10-6

COPYRIGHT © 1999 CORE KNOWLEDGE FOUNDATION

ALL RIGHTS RESERVED

PRINTED IN CANADA

7 TH PRINTING

COVER ILLUSTRATION BY GB MACINTOSH

ILLUSTRATIONS BY GUSTAVE DORE (1832-1883)

CORE KNOWLEDGE FOUNDATION

801 EAST HIGH STREET

CHARLOTTESVILLE, VIRGINIA 22902

www.coreknowledge.org

TABLE OF CONTENTS

TABLE OF CONTENTS

PART TWO

Introduction

THERE IS A STORY THAT THE KING OF SPAIN ONCE looked out a window onto the street and saw a man walking along reading a book, slapping his head and roaring with laughter. "I'll bet he is reading *Don Quixote*," the king exclaimed.

It certainly would have pleased Miguel de Cervantes if the king won such a wager, because Cervantes meant for people to laugh as they read his book. Doctors in his day believed that the cure for melancholy, a feeling of sadness that we often call depression, was to laugh out loud a lot. Cervantes also wanted readers to see that a sense of humor makes it easier to cope with life's disappointments and people's faults.

Besides wanting to make people laugh, Cervantes said he also wrote to rid people of their taste for romances, those fantastic stories about bold knights and fair damsels, evil giants and sorcerers, dragons and quests. But even though Cervantes said he disliked romances because they gave people foolish ideas, it is clear he was fond of them himself.

Romances tried to uphold the ideals of chivalry, a medieval code of behavior for knights that gave an air of nobility and grandeur to all the unlikely events these tales told. The knights who were the stories' heroes were tested in ordeals, most often in combat, and their success was a proof of their virtue and honor. Some who roved in search of adventure (they were called knights-errant) sought ordeals that tested just themselves. The knight's devotion to a maiden was tested, too, to prove his self-control and patience. Thus, the more a knight suffered in love and waited to be accepted by the maiden, the more he proved his feeling was true.

That is all fine in the world imagined in a book, according to Cervantes, but try living that way in the everyday world and you'll seem crazy. This points out the difference between a romance and a novel: a romance describes uncommon things that almost certainly couldn't be true, whereas a novel describes ordinary things so convincingly that one believes the story actually could have happened. Some people say *Don Quixote* is the first modern novel because it put the events of a romance into ordinary settings, and so made their outcomes funny, and also because its main character is not a superhero but an ordinary man whom readers grow to understand and even admire.

Don Quixote is one of the most famous characters in literature. His name has become a word, "quixotic," that means to do something foolishly impractical for the sake of a high ideal. Equally famous is his companion Sancho Panza. As Don Quixote wanders Spain thinking of himself as a storybook knight-errant, Sancho takes the role of the knight's loyal squire. Don Quixote is idealistic and intelligent, but crazy, because he is living in the everyday world but believing it is the world of romances. He is too old and weak to be a knight-errant, but he doesn't think so. Sancho has solid common sense and sees everyday reality clearly, but he is ignorant and willing to lie. He knows it is useless to try to reason with madmen and so he plays along, hoping to find a profit in it. Cervantes seems to wish we could mix the best qualities of this knight and squire in ourselves; then we would see our everyday selves as we truly are and still strive to be nobler and better.

Cervantes' great novel, so wise about human nature and so loving in telling the plain truth about it, was a sensational success. It was well known even before it was printed, because his friends who had read its handwritten pages could not help sharing its funny episodes with others. Since its first publication in 1605, *Don Quixote* has been translated into more languages than any other book ever written except the Bible.

E. D. HIRSCH, JR.
CHARLOTTESVILLE, VIRGINIA

The Adventures of
Don Quixote

PART *1*

THIS ELDERLY GENTLEMAN READ ROMANCES
OF CHIVALRY WITH ARDOR AND INTENSITY.

CHAPTER I

An Old-School Gentleman Gone Mad

ONCE UPON A TIME THERE LIVED IN A VILLAGE IN SPAIN, in the province of La Mancha, one of those gentlemen of the old school who keep an ancient lance and shield hung up in their hall, and maintain a riding horse and a hunting dog. About three-fourths of the income of this particular gentleman went in household expenses. The remainder served to keep him in decent clothes, with a best suit for Sundays and holidays, and one of good **homespun** for everyday use. His household

HOMESPUN
Loosely woven fabric, usually wool or linen, made from yarn spun at home.

consisted of an elderly housekeeper, a niece of his under twenty, and a handyman who could help in the house or outdoors and was equally good at saddling the horse or wielding the pruning knife.

Our gentleman was about fifty, thin, but tough of body, with a lean face, a very early riser, and a great lover of hunting. His name was Quixania.

This elderly gentleman got into the habit of reading romances of **chivalry** with such ardor and intensity that at last he lost interest in hunting and even neglected his daily concerns. He became so passionate about the subject that he even sold several acres of good cropland in order to buy as many books about chivalry as he could lay his hands on. He passed whole days and nights studying the preposterous adventures of Don Belianis, Amadis of Gaul and other knights, until at last his brain became so agitated and his judgment so warped, that he resolved to become a knight himself and ride about the world setting wrongs right and seeking adventures.

CHIVALRY
The ideals of medieval knights that emphasized gallantry, honor and courtesy, especially toward women. The stories of knights whose adventures illustrated the spirit of chivalry were called romances.

The first thing he did was polish up some old armor that had belonged to his ancestors and had lain for ages in a corner, covered with dust and rust. Having cleaned and adjust-

THE FIRST THING HE DID WAS POLISH UP SOME OLD ARMOR.

ed them as best he could, he found he had one great deficiency. There was no helmet, only a simple steel cap. However, his ingenuity soon made up for this defect. By means of some cardboard he made a visor that, fixed to the cap, gave the appearance of being a complete helmet. Unfortunately, he got the idea to test its strength for resisting cuts, and so, drawing his sword, he made a stroke at it and in one instant demolished the work that had taken a whole week. Deciding to make something stronger, he got strips of iron and made them a lining to the cardboard. He then declared his new visor was sufficiently strong, without risking any more experiments on it.

He next turned his attention to his horse, and though this animal had as many points as a mariner's compass, and was only skin and bone, it appeared to him to be a charger superior to the **Bucephalus of Alexander**.

BUCEPHALUS OF ALEXANDER
Legendary for his speed and courage, Bucephalus was the favorite horse of Alexander the Great, the conqueror of the ancient world. After Bucephalus died of battle wounds, at the old age of 30, Alexander founded a city named for him in what is now Pakistan.

He spent four days considering what he should name this wonderful animal. He said to himself that it would not be proper that the horse of so famous a knight as he was going to be, and an animal itself so excellent, should be without a worthy name. He therefore sought a name that would indicate at once what the horse was and what it had been. After making up and rejecting many possible names, he at last fixed on "Rocinante."

To his thinking, it was a lofty and resonant name, and it sig-
nified that the horse that before had been a
mere **hack** was now the foremost of all
the hacks in the world.

Having given his horse a name
so much to his taste, he wanted a new
one for himself, too. He thought about it
for eight days more and at last decided in
favor of Don Quixote. Remembering that
the valiant Amadis did not call himself simply Amadis, but added the name of his coun-
try to it, so Don Quixote wished to enlarge his name to Don
Quixote de la Mancha. Thereby, he judged, he made clear his
origin and honored his country by adopting its name.

HACK
A horse hired
out for any use
and generally
worn out from
hard work.

He saw nothing left to do but to find a lady to be in
love with, for a knight-errant without a lady-love was like a
tree without leaves or fruit, or a body without a soul. "For," he
said to himself, "if on account of my sins, or by good fortune,
I should meet a giant (which is a common occurrence for
knights) and cut him in two, or in some way vanquish him, it
would be well to have some lady to whom I could order him
to present himself. On his arrival he would throw himself on
his knees before the fair one, and say in a humble voice, 'I,
lady, am the giant Caraculiambro, who has been vanquished

in single combat by Don Quixote de la Mancha, who can never be too highly praised, and who has commanded me to present myself before your ladyship in order that you may dispose of me as you please.'" The idea pleased him greatly.

In his own neighborhood there was a very good-looking farmer's daughter whom he had once been smitten with, though she did not seem to know or care anything about him. Her name was Aldonza Lorenzo and he thought her fit to be the lady of his heart. He sought for a name for her that would be suggestive of a princess. In the end he called her Dulcinea del Toboso (since she was a native of Toboso), a name that seemed to him musical and significant, like all the others he had adopted.

Everything now being ready, and thinking the world might suffer if he were tardy, he lost no time in starting on his mission. One morning before daybreak, on one of the hottest days in July, he donned his armor, mounted Rocinante, stole away through a private gate of his yard and reached open country, greatly pleased with how easily he had begun.

But his joy was short-lived. He suddenly remembered he had not been dubbed a knight in the proper form and that, according to the laws of chivalry, he had no right to wear anything but **white armor,** nor to carry a **device** on his shield until he had earned one through his exploits. So great was his concern at this discovery that he almost turned back. But, reflecting that this would not mend matters and his folly overcoming every other impulse, he continued on, resolving to get himself knighted by the first knight he should come across, according to examples in books he had read. As to the white armor, he would scour his own so that it would be whiter than ermine. Having satisfied his mind in this way, he allowed his horse to follow whatever road it pleased, considering this to be the true spirit of adventure.

WHITE ARMOR
A young man about to be made a knight first confessed all his past deeds and then he put on a white tunic to symbolize his purity on entering into the order of chivalry. The ceremony conferring knighthood had similarities to the Christian ritual of baptism.

They jogged along all day, Don Quixote glorying in thoughts of what future historians would say of him, and in the meantime suffering enough intense heat from the sun to melt his brains, if he had any. Night approached without any adventure. As both horse and rider were quite worn out and almost dead from hunger, Don Quixote began to look for a castle, or a shepherd's hut, where he could find food and rest. At last he saw an inn not far from the road and reached it just before nightfall. By the door there stood a couple of young wenches,

DEVICE
The design or emblem a knight chose that identified him, often his family crest.

who were on their way to **Seville** and stopping for the night at the inn.

Now, as everything he thought, saw or imagined was tinted and transformed by the nonsense he gathered from his books of chivalry, he at once pictured this inn as a castle with four towers, spires of polished silver, a drawbridge and moat, and all the usual features of castles in romances. Pulling up his steed a little distance away, he waited for a dwarf or **page** to announce his arrival by the blast of a trumpet from the battlements. But finding there was some unexplained delay, and Rocinante being impatient to get to the stable, he advanced nearer the door. There he caught sight of the two girls already mentioned, who appeared to him to be two beautiful damsels.

SEVILLE
The chief city of southern Spain. Long held by the Moors, it was a center of learning and the capital of bullfighting.

PAGE
A youth in training for knighthood who is a personal servant to a knight.

Just then it happened that a pig-driver blew on his horn to call his herd from a nearby field. At once Don Quixote recognized this as the signal of his arrival. So, with extreme self-satisfaction, he approached the ladies, who at the sight of a man so strangely outfitted and bearing a lance and shield, became alarmed and turned to go indoors. But Don Quixote gracefully raised his cardboard visor, revealing his lean, dusty face, and in soothing tones addressed them.

"Do not fly, gentle ladies, and do not be in the least uneasy, for it would ill become a member of the order of chivalry, to which I belong, to do wrong to anyone, let alone such exalted young ladies as your appearance indicates you to be."

The girls were astonished and amused at being addressed in this fashion, but not as surprised as the landlord, a fat, good-natured fellow who just then came out to receive his odd-looking guest. He helped him down, attended to his wants and those of Rocinante, and in the course of conversation readily made out the kind of madness from which the stranger suffered. The host happened to know a great deal about the romances of knights-errant and he could not resist the chance to play along with the folly of Don Quixote in order to amuse himself and his guests, who were mostly passing herdsmen and mule drivers.

As soon as Don Quixote had satisfied his hunger, he approached the innkeeper, and, falling on his knees before him, begged him in very flowery language to dub him a knight. His lordship graciously agreed, but reminded Don Quixote that he must first pass a night watching his armor.

DON QUIXOTE BEGGED HIM IN VERY FLOWERY
LANGUAGE TO DUB HIM A KNIGHT.

Don Quixote then asked to be taken to the chapel to lay his armor in front of the altar. The host explained that the chapel had recently been demolished so that it might be rebuilt, and suggested that the ceremony take place in the courtyard. Such a thing might be done in cases of necessity, he said, as was recorded in the histories of famous knights.

So Don Quixote removed his armor and put it in a trough in one of the yards of the inn. For hours he marched up and down in front of it, lance in hand, in the bright moon-light, to the amusement of the landlord and his friends.

It happened, as the night wore on, that one of the mule drivers came into the yard to fetch water for his mules and was unfortunate enough to lay hands on the armor in order to move it. He had hardly done so when the vigilant Don Quixote gave him such a thwack on the head with his lance that he was knocked out. Then the knight calmly continued his march until a second mule driver, on the same errand, approached the trough and began handling the armor. The second driver promptly met the same fate as the first one.

The comrades of the injured men, coming to learn what was going on, rushed into the yard in anger and began pelting the knight with anything they could pick up. Don Quixote bravely stood his ground, sheltering himself with his shield as best he could and hurling defiance and threats back. How the fight might have ended is impossible to say, had it not been for the arrival of the landlord. Fearing that he was responsible for letting the joke go too far, he anxiously called on the drivers to stop their attack, reminding them that they were dealing with a madman who would not be held account-able for his actions, even if he killed some of them.

In this way the tumult came to an end. The landlord next considered how he could speedily get rid of his danger-

FOR HOURS HE MARCHED UP AND DOWN
IN THE BRIGHT MOONLIGHT.

ous guest. He decided the best and safest way would be to hurry through a ceremony of knighting. He persuaded Don Quixote that his vigil had lasted long enough and proceeded hastily with the formalities. He brought out the account book he kept track of his hay and barley in and pretended to read prayers from it over the kneeling knight. He rapped him twice on the shoulders and neck pretty sharply and declared him a member of the order of chivalry. The two girls then buckled on his sword and spurs and wished him success in battle. Don Quixote gracefully responded, mounted his gallant steed, took a courteous farewell of the lord and ladies of the castle and sallied forth in quest of new adventures. The landlord thought it best not to ask for what he was owed.

DON QUIXOTE CALLED ON THE MAN TO
STOP OR FACE INSTANT DEATH.

CHAPTER 2

The New Knight's First Adventures

I T WAS DAYBREAK WHEN DON QUIXOTE RODE AWAY FROM the inn, proud of being a full-fledged knight. Reflecting, however, that he still lacked a squire, a necessary assistant to a knight, and remembering that he had a man at home—a very honest and simple fellow—whom he could probably enlist in this service, he turned his horse's head in the direction of his native village.

He had not gone very far when he was startled by loud cries of distress from a forest a little distance away. Riding at once in that direction, he came upon a strange scene. He saw a stout lad of about fifteen tied to a tree, stripped to his waist. A burly farmer was thrashing him unmercifully with a strap. Don Quixote commandingly called on the man to stop or face instant death, and the farmer, daunted by this sudden sight, did so at once. In apologetic tones, he explained that the boy was an habitually idle servant of his, who, instead of looking after the sheep entrusted to him, was constantly losing one or more of them, and therefore was getting correction. The youth, however, said his master was looking for an excuse to cheat him of the wages he was due.

Don Quixote, without hearing more, sided with the boy and commanded his master to release him at once and pay what he owed him, which appeared to be sixty-three **reals** for nine month's service. The man obeyed without a word, untied the youth, and promised to pay him what he was due, and even more, if he would come home with him, since he did not have money with him. The boy protested that if his master got him in his clutches again, he would flay him like **St. Bartholomew**. To answer this, Don Quixote decided that the farmer should swear by the order of chivalry to pay the boy honestly and let him go free without further harm. The farmer was willing to swear this oath, or any

REALS
A silver coin about the size of a quarter once used in Spain and its possessions.

ST. BARTHOLOMEW
One of the 12 apostles of Jesus, sent by him to spread the Christian religion. St. Bartholomew preached in Asia Minor, Persia, and India. He was tortured to death in Armenia by having his skin torn off while still alive and then being beheaded.

other, to get rid of the knight, and so the matter was decided, in spite of the youth's loud objections that the farmer would certainly not keep his promise. Don Quixote could not imagine such wickedness, but warned the farmer that he was dealing with the Knight of La Mancha, the righter of wrongs, who would return and punish him harshly if he failed in any detail of his promise. Satisfied with that, he put his spurs to Rocinante and rode rapidly away.

The farmer watched the knight until he was out of sight, and when he saw the coast was clear he turned to the lad and said, "Come here, my son, and I will pay you what I owe you, as the good gentleman commanded me." With that he grabbed the boy, tied him to the tree again, and whipped him within an inch of his life. "Now," he said, "you can call on your knight and see if he can wipe that out. I have a good mind to skin you alive, just as you said I would." However, he let the youngster go and urged him to seek justice from his champion. The boy vowed he would, but apparently he never succeeded.

Meanwhile the knight, having covered miles of road on his way home, saw a company of men coming towards him. They were six silk merchants riding to **Murcia** with four mounted servants and three mule drivers on foot. Don Quixote instantly identified

MURCIA
A province of Spain on its Mediterreanean coast.

them as knights with their squires and servants. Pleased with the good work he had done with the farmer, he decided to make this an occasion for proving his new knighthood. So he planted himself in the middle of the road with his lance raised

and his shield in position, just as he had read in books of chivalry.

When the party came within hail, he called out in a defiant tone, "Halt, every one of you, until each of you swears there is not in the whole world a more beautiful lady than the Empress of La Mancha, Dulcinea del Toboso."

The merchants stopped, wondering what sort of escaped lunatic this figure might be. To humor him, however, one stepped forward and said, "Sir knight, none of us are acquainted with the lady you mention, but if you show her to us, no doubt we shall be able to agree with you."

"And what would be the use of that?" argued Don Quixote. "That would be nothing but admitting the obvious. The important point is that, without seeing her, you affirm it and mean it. If you refuse, I challenge you to combat, all haughty and overbearing as you are. You can come at me one at a time, as the rules of chivalry direct, or you can come all at once, as is the custom with those of your low breeding. I am ready and waiting, confident in the justice of my cause."

"But sir," pleaded the amused merchant, "I beg you in the name of all the princes here that you not burden our consciences by forcing us to confess something we have no knowledge of, and which so much insults the lovely Queens of Alcarria and Estramadura. Show us at least some picture, however small, of the lady, so that we may have some excuse for doing as you wish. Indeed, I say for all of us that we are so anxious to oblige you that we would declare her all you say she is even if the portrait showed her to be squint-eyed and humpbacked!"

ONE OF THE MULE DRIVERS PROCEEDED
TO BEAT HIM IN A BRUTAL FASHION.

At these suggestions Don Quixote boiled with rage. "She is neither squint-eyed nor humpbacked, you dogs! You will pay for the outrageous blasphemy you have uttered against a beauty so rare as that of my lady."

Saying this, he leveled his lance and charged the spokesman of the group, for whom things might have gone badly, except that Rocinante stumbled and rolled with his master over and over on the ground. Don Quixote, weighed down with his ancient armor and hindered by his weapons and spurs, was unable to get up, in spite of all his efforts. He kept calling to the merchants not to leave like cowards, but to wait until he could get back on his horse.

The merchants paid no attention to his ravings and went on their way. But one of the mule drivers, a violent, bad-tempered fellow, resented the knight's insults and, first smashing the lance in pieces, proceeded to beat him with a stave of it in a most brutal fashion. At length the fellow gave in to the repeated calls of the merchants to come along and left the poor fallen gentleman half dead on the road, less able to get up than ever. There Don Quixote lay, bruised and almost unconscious, comforting himself with thoughts about similar misfortunes that happened to other knights, and reciting in a feeble voice what he could remember of their poetic words as they lay wounded and abandoned on the field of battle.

As he was going on in this way, a countryman who happened to be from the same village came along, who, seeing a fellow creature in such obvious suffering, began to help him as much as he could. He soon discovered that the battered man was no other than his neighbor Don Quixote. With some difficulty he lifted him on his mule and led the animal and Rocinante by the bridles toward the village, much concerned with the knight's rambling talk and the difficulty of keeping him from falling on the road again.

HE LED THE ANIMALS BY THEIR
BRIDLES TOWARD THE VILLAGE.

Arriving after nightfall at Don Quixote's house, he explained how he found him lying on the road and handed him over to the care of the housekeeper and niece, who, along with the parish priest and the village barber, were just then earnestly discussing Don Quixote's six-day absence. They were glad to see him home again, though shocked at his sad condition. Since they could get nothing from him except wild ravings about confronting ten enormous giants, they put him to bed, where he soon sank into a long and deep sleep.

That night all four unanimously resolved to destroy the books that had been so instrumental in befuddling the brain of the unfortunate gentleman. So they picked out all the books of chivalry from Don Quixote's library, threw them out the window into the courtyard, and made a bonfire of them. That was not enough. They took the extra precaution of walling-up the door to the library, feeling sure the knight could be persuaded that the room and its books had vanished by magic. Indeed, some days later, when that excuse had to be made, Don Quixote accepted it easily and at once declared that the disappearance was the work of his archenemy, the powerful magician Freston.

For fifteen days Don Quixote was nursed by his friends, recovering strength in his body and calmness in his

HE PROMISED HIM THE GOVERNORSHIP OF AN ISLAND.

mind, though he occasionally showed signs of still being afflict-
ed with his peculiar craze. After that time, when he was able to
move about and go outdoors, he began meddling privately
with the man he had thought about as a squire, a simple-mind-
ed and gullible laborer named Sancho Panza. He promised
him all kinds of benefits, particularly that he would reward
him with the governorship of a province or island at the end of
their great adventure. By such enticements he won Sancho's
consent to his wild scheme. The knight next set about raising
money for the expenses of repairing and replacing his armor

and weapons and all the necessary preparations for a fresh expedition as a full-blown knight-errant.

A problem arose over a mount for the new squire, who had only a donkey to ride on. Don Quixote tried in vain to remember any mention in the books he had read about a squire being so mounted. In the end he decided to make do with the donkey until a better animal could be had by seizing it from the first rude knight he might encounter.

Everything being arranged, Don Quixote and his squire stole away in the middle of the night, unknown to anyone, and by daybreak were far enough away to be safe from interference from their friends.

They followed the route Don Quixote had originally taken, talking for a long time about the circumstances under which a knight-errant was able to grant a governorship, or even a kingdom, to his squire. Sancho Panza was mightily well pleased.

They were still talking when they came in sight of thirty or forty windmills in the plain before them. Seeing them, Don Quixote shouted, "Chance has brought us better luck than we could have hoped for. See there, Sancho, thirty or more enormous giants! I shall attack and destroy them all, and we shall be rich with their **spoils**, as is legal

SPOILS
Property taken from an enemy in war or a victim in a robbery; loot.

in warfare, and, in addition, it is a service to God to rid the world of such an evil race."

"What giants?" asked Sancho.

"Those with the great arms," answered his master.

"Why, your honor," said Sancho, "those are not giants, but only windmills, and what you call arms are the sails, which, being turned by the wind, cause the millstones to work."

"It is evident," replied Don Quixote, "that you are not experienced in adventures of this sort. They are giants surely enough, and if you are afraid you had better go back a little distance while I engage them in fearful and unequal battle."

So saying, the knight spurred on Rocinante, ignoring the cries of his squire, who warned him that he was indeed attacking windmills. But so fixed was Don Quixote on the idea that they were giants that he would not listen to his squire or see with his own eyes what was plain enough in front of him. Forward he went, yelling, "Fly not, cowards and scoundrels! It is only a solitary knight who attacks you."

Just then the wind rose a little and the great sails of the windmill began to revolve. Don Quixote shouted out, "Though you wave more arms than **Briares**, you will still answer to me." And commending himself to his lady Dulcinea, he charged at a full gallop against the nearest windmill. The lance passed

BRIARES
A mythological giant who had one hundred arms.

THE LANCE PASSED THROUGH THE SAIL, WHICH CAUGHT IT.

through the sail, which caught it and broke it, but not before Don Quixote and his steed were dragged up with it and then thrown down on the ground some distance away.

Sancho Panza rushed to help, exclaiming, "Bless the Lord! Did I not tell your worship these were only windmills? And no one could mistake them for anything else unless he had something like them in his own head!"

"Silence, Sancho!" replied Don Quixote, slowly recovering from his injuries. "In war, things are strangely liable to sudden changes. Indeed, even more so than I supposed. It is clear that the crafty Freston, who stole my library, changed the giants into windmills in order to cheat me of the glory of defeating them. Such is his hatred of me, but in the end his tricks will be useless against the power of my sword!"

"As God pleases," answered Sancho Panza, as he busied himself putting his master and Rocinante back in condition to continue their journey. They had not gone far when Sancho remarked that it seemed to be near dinnertime. Don Quixote replied that he did not feel hungry just then, but Sancho might eat whenever he pleased. With this permission, the squire arranged himself as well as he could on the back of his donkey. Taking some provisions from his pouch, he began to eat with great satisfaction, drinking long and often from a flask of wine he carried. On the whole, he thought it was pleasant enough to go about the country seeking adventures, even if they might be dangerous to others.

CHAPTER 3

More Thrilling Adventures: The Captive Princess and Blanket-tossing

THEY RESTED THAT NIGHT AMONG SOME TREES A SHORT distance off the high road. The knight thought it his duty to behave like the knights of the romances, who often stayed awake thinking about their lady-loves. But Sancho, after his hearty meal and all the wine he drank, fell asleep at once and did not awake until his sleepless master roused him in full daylight. Don Quixote did not want breakfast. Sancho helped himself to food, noticing with a sigh that the wine flask was becoming very light. The two then struck out again on the public highway leading to Puerto Lapice.

In the afternoon they found themselves approaching a couple of monks from the **Order of St. Benedict** with hoods over their faces and umbrellas in their hands, each mounted on a big, magnificent mule. A little behind them, but not in their party, came a coach containing a lady from **Biscay** and her maid on their way to Seville to join the lady's husband, who was going to the Indies to take an important post. The coach was accompanied by four or five mounted men and two mule drivers.

ORDER OF ST. BENEDICT
A religious order of the Catholic Church whose rules for monastic living are moderate, stressing prayer and manual labor. Benedictines wear black robes.

BISCAY
The Basque provinces of northern Spain where the natives, famous for their fierce independence, speak Basque and Spanish is spoken with a different accent.

No sooner did Don Quixote see the travelers than he said to Sancho, "I am much mistaken if this is not going to be one of the most famous adventures ever known. These masked men in front are no doubt sorcerers who are carrying off the coach of some grand princess, and it is my clear duty to prevent them by all means in my power."

"Why," said Sancho, "this is worse than the windmills. Do you not see that the men in front are Benedictine friars and the coach is probably that of some gentleman? Mind what you are doing, sir, and do not let the devil deceive you!"

"I have already remarked, friend Sancho, that you know nothing of the nature of knightly adventures. You will soon see that what I have told you is correct."

With that, he planted himself in the middle of the road with a commanding attitude and called out to the monks, "Diabolical beings, release the princess you are carrying off in that coach or prepare to die!"

The friars dropped their reins and stopped, amazed by the figure before them and its strange speech.

"Good sir," said one of them at last, "we are not diabolical beings, but brothers of the Order of St. Benedict, who are journeying on the business of our monastery. As for the coach behind us, we know nothing of it, nor can we tell if it contains a captive princess or not."

"No bandying soft words with me, you scoundrels." cried Don Quixote. "I know well who you are!" And without more ado he charged the foremost monk, who, if he had not gracefully and promptly fallen off his mule, would have been knocked off in a very unpleasant fashion. The other monk

HE PLANTED HIMSELF IN THE MIDDLE OF THE ROAD
WITH A COMMANDING ATTITUDE.

thought it wise to use his heels on the sides of his beast and flew off over the plain as fast as the wind itself.

Don Quixote trotted on to meet the coach, and Sancho dismounted and began to strip the fallen monk. As he was doing this, two mule drivers of the monks came up and asked what he was doing. Sancho said he was gathering the spoils of battle won by his master. The men, who understood nothing of battle or spoils, and taking the matter seriously, fell upon Sancho instantly, pulling out his beard by the handfuls and giving him such a kicking that he was left breathless on the ground. They then lifted the fallen monk on his mule and went off to join the monk who had fled, who was waiting at a safe distance. Once reunited, the friars hastened on their way, **crossing themselves** as if the devil were behind them.

Meanwhile, Don Quixote had ceremoniously introduced himself to the lady of the coach and added, "Your highness is now free to do as you please, for I have vanquished your wicked captors by the might of my arm. In payment of this service, all I ask of you is that you turn around and go to Toboso, and there report to Lady Dulcinea all I have done for you."

CROSSING THEMSELVES
A gesture, called the sign of the cross, made by Roman Catholic, Eastern Orthodox and Anglican Christians, that traces the shape of a cross between the forehead, breast and shoulders to remember Jesus' death on the cross and to ask for God's blessing.

The lady's Biscayan attendants could not make out what the knight was saying, but gathered that they were now expected to journey out of their way to Toboso. One, impatient and hot-tempered, went up to the knight and, pushing aside his lance, said in broken Spanish, "Clear out of the way, sir, and let the coach and lady alone, or, as sure as I am Basque, I will knock the life out of you."

To this Don Quixote calmly replied, "If you were a gentleman—which you are not—I would punish you for your

THEY ATTACKED EACH OTHER, SLASHING AND MANEUVERING.

rashness. But I cannot bother with such a miserable creature as you."

At this the Biscayan flamed up and roared out that he was of good birth and ancient blood, and that he was a gentleman by land or sea and everywhere and at all times. He would prove it if Don Quixote would throw down his lance and take to his sword.

The knight accepted the challenge, drew his sword and prepared to slay the Biscayan for his insolence. The valiant Biscayan drew his sword and took a cushion from the coach to be his shield. Still, he had the disadvantage of riding a slow, stupid mule while Don Quixote was mounted on Rocinante, who was more manageable.

They attacked each other with great ferocity, slashing and maneuvering, raising a great cloud of dust, but doing little harm to each other. At last, however, the Biscayan struck home a heavy blow on Don Quixote, which would have ended the knight's life if it had not been somewhat deflected by his shield. As it was, the blow chopped away the left side of his helmet and half of his ear, and fell on his shoulder with such force that it almost knocked him out of his saddle. Quickly recovering himself and now more furious than ever, Don Quixote readied himself for one tremendous blow that should end the battle. Grasping his sword with both hands, and calling loudly for Lady Dulcinea's protection, he raised his sword over the doomed Biscayan–doomed because at that critical moment, when his only chance of escape was to swerve, his mule refused to move. Down came the mighty sword of the knight on the head of the Biscayan, which was guarded only by the cushion, and in a moment he lay sprawling in the dust, bleeding from his nose, mouth and ears.

Don Quixote jumped down from his steed and, with his sword on the man's throat, called on him to surrender or die. But the unfortunate fellow did not have the power to speak and would have suffered the consequences of silence if the ladies in the coach (who had been watching in terror) had not come out and begged the knight to spare his life. Don Quixote graciously agreed to do so, on the condition that the man go to Toboso and submit to the will of the Princess Dulcinea. The poor ladies gave their pledge, without understanding in the least what the whole business was about. But this was enough for Don Quixote, who rode away, followed by Sancho Panza.

As they rode along, Sancho cautiously asked if the success of the battle could mean his appointment as governor of an island. Don Quixote explained that such trivial encounters on the road did not lead to governorships, or, indeed, anything better than broken heads and chopped-off ears. Sancho must be patient until more serious adventures arose; then there would be no shortage of governorships to choose from.

Meanwhile the knight's injured ear continued to bleed freely. Sancho proposed that they stop to bandage it. Don Quixote expressed regret that he did not have some wonderful **balsam of the great Fierabas**, a single drop of which would cure the most serious wounds. However, he knew the recipe by heart and would make it on the first opportunity he got. "It is

BALSAM OF THE GREAT FIERABAS
Balsam is a fragrant resin from a tree, such as a fir, used in medicines and perfumes. According to legend, Fierabas was a giant who stole from Rome the liquid with which Jesus had been embalmed, which was believed to have the power to miraculously heal wounds.

a balsam that heals wounds that are otherwise mortal," he said, "and therefore, when I have given it to your charge, all you will have to do when I am cut in two in some battle (as is often the case) is take the two pieces before the blood has a chance to congeal, place then very exactly next to one another, give me two drinks of the liquid and you will see me instantly become as sound as an apple."

Sancho promised to keep this in mind. He was deeply impressed with the miraculous powers of the liquid and suggested that he be given the recipe as payment on the promise of a governorship, for he knew he could make a fortune from it. But his master would not listen to such a greedy proposal. For the time being, Sancho treated the injured ear with lint and ointment he carried in his pouch.

After a meal of bread and onions, as darkness came on, they made haste to find a place where they could lodge for the night. They came upon nothing but the huts of some goatherds, where they were kindly received and treated to a hot supper of goat meat. They passed the night in conversation with the goatherds and were entertained by the long history of the cruel fate of one Chrysostom, a young shepherd who had died that morning of a broken heart for the love of a girl who spurned him. Don Quixote was so interested in this touching story that he went with the goatherds to the young man's

DON QUIXOTE COULD TRAVEL ONLY IN
A SLOW, PAINFUL FASHION.

funeral the next day. After the melancholy ceremony, the knight and his squire went on their way.

The day promised to be uneventful, and would have been but for the frolics of Rocinante among a drove of horses as his master and Sancho napped in the shade of some trees. The drovers, who numbered about twenty, beat off Rocinante with needless violence. Don Quixote, awakening and seeing how his steed was being treated, did not hesitate to seek revenge. The fight was short and sharp, as might be expected from the difference in numbers, and both the knight and squire were left badly bruised by the staffs of the drovers, who also gave poor Rocinante added blows.

It was a long time before Don Quixote and his horse could travel, and then only in a slow and painful fashion. Late in the day they limped as far as a roadside inn, where their battered condition caused great excitement and sympathy in the compassionate landlady and her daughter, who plastered Don Quixote's bruises. Rickety beds in the attic were the best sleeping accommodation that could be provided. Don Quixote, however, fancied that he was in a castle.

In the middle of the night, his injuries began to be painful again and, remembering the balsam of Fierabas, he called out to Sancho: "Rise, Sancho, if you can, and call upon the governor of this castle to supply you oil, wine, salt and rosemary to make the healing balsam, for in truth I want it badly."

Sancho, stiff and sore himself, blundered about in the dark but at last found the landlord and got what he needed. He gave them to Don Quixote, who mixed portions together, put them in a pot over the fire and boiled them down to what he judged to be the proper consistency. Having prayed and made many crosses over the pot, he filled a flask for future use and then drank down about a pint and a half of what was left.

The result was immediate and startling. The stuff caused a most violent attack of retching, which emptied the knight's stomach of everything it held in a brief time. Then Don Quixote began to sweat very heavily, so that he had to be covered up to stay warm, and finally he fell into a deep sleep. After three hours he woke up, hardly feeling any pain from his bruises. He was now firmly convinced that with such a remedy he could take any risk on the field of battle without danger from wounds, regardless of how serious they might be.

Sancho, seeing the good the balsam had done his master, begged to try it. Permission was granted and he drank what was left in the pot, which was nearly as much as the knight had taken. But the medicine did not work in the same way. Perhaps because of his delicate stomach, it stayed inside him, causing the most horrible cramps and bringing on a series of cold sweats, shiverings and faintings, until he thought his fatal hour had come. At last relief came, though in a violent and volcanic manner at both ends, and left him quite exhausted.

The knight, on the contrary, was ready to be off and felt himself in prime condition for his chivalrous duties. He saddled Rocinante himself, took a **pike** he found in the yard to be his lance, vaulted into the saddle, and

PIKE
A weapon used by foot soldiers that had a long shaft topped by cutting edges.

THE MEDICINE DID NOT WORK

IN THE SAME WAY.

from that perch gave a flowery speech to twenty or so people who had come out of the inn to watch him. The innkeeper stepped forward to remind him that he had not paid his bill.

"What!" cried Don Quixote. "Is this really an inn? I took it for a castle. But inn or castle, it is against my principles to pay anything. Whoever heard of a knight-errant being called upon to pay for his lodgings?"

The landlord protested that he knew nothing about such principles and only wanted what was owed to him. But Don Quixote, calling him a fool and a miserable innkeeper, spurred Rocinante, brandished his pike, and scornfully rode away. No one tried to stop him.

The innkeeper, seeing the master ride off, went indoors to find Sancho. But when Sancho heard where matters stood, he flatly refused to go against his master's principle and swore he would not pay a penny. The other guests at the inn sympathized with the landlord and some of the lively ones decided he should get justice.

Getting a stout blanket, they put Sancho in it and carried him to the yard, where they tossed him high in the air amid shouts and roars of laughter. Don Quixote, hearing the uproar and noticing that his squire was not with him, rode back to the inn. There he heard the protesting voice of his faithful squire and caught brief glimpses of his grotesque out-

THEY TOSSED HIM HIGH IN THE AIR AMID

SHOUTS AND ROARS OF LAUGHTER.

lines as he rose in the air above the wall of the yard. In a great
rage, Don Quixote rode around the inn trying to find a way in
to rescue Sancho, but all the gates had been locked. The knight
was reduced to making threats of revenge. But none of these
had any effect on those in the yard. They did not stop laughing or tossing until they were finally tired out. Then they sat
Sancho on his donkey and rushed him out a partly open gate,
which they immediately closed again.

CHAPTER 4

Hostile Armies, More Magic and the Spoils of Victory

ANCHO JOINED HIS MASTER AND ONCE MORE THEY RODE together. To cheer up Sancho, Don Quixote remarked, "Sancho, I am now convinced that yonder castle or inn, whatever it may be, is enchanted. And those we had to deal with there are spirits from another world."

Sancho was in no mood to be comforted with philosophical speculations of this kind. He refused to accept them, saying, to the contrary, they were men of flesh and blood like themselves, as he found out to his pain. But, men or spirits, in view of their many misadventures, he thought it was about time to return home, especially as it was now almost harvest time. The knight would not hear of it, and they were still arguing the point when they noticed a cloud of dust rolling towards them on the road.

"See that cloud of dust," said the knight. "It is caused by a great army made of many nations."

"Then there must be two armies," said the squire, "because here on the other side is a similar cloud of dust."

Don Quixote turned around, saw such was the case, and declared they were hostile armies about to engage in battle on that vast plain. Not only that, he also began to explain what the quarrel was about, who the leaders on each side were, how they had performed in the past, what banners they carried, and what the devices on their shields meant. He bewildered poor Sancho with such names as the Emperor Alifanfaron, the King Pentapolin, the brave Laurcalo, the giant Microcolembo, and many other persons. Sancho listened to all this in silence, but with perplexity, as the clouds of dust came nearer. He could catch glimpses of what they held, and at length he said, "Sir, perhaps this may be another case of enchantment."

"What!" replied his master. "Cannot you at least hear the neighing of the warhorses, the sound of the trumpets, and the rattling of the drums?"

"Why, I do hear something now," Sancho answered. "But it sounds very like the bleating of sheep and the shouting of shepherds."

"Your fear, Sancho, prevents you from hearing right," said Don Quixote, "so be off to a safe distance while I go adjust the balance of right and wrong between the two enemies."

As the knight rode off on his mission, Sancho, seeing more than before, called after him: "Stop, sir! Stop! Come back! They are only lambs and sheep. Woe to me that I was born. What new madness is this?"

But Don Quixote rode on, calling aloud, "Ho! Knights of the valiant Emperor Pentapolin of the Naked Arm, follow me and see how I avenge you on Alifanfaron of Zoprobana!" Saying this, he rushed into the cloud of dust and began spearing lambs and sheep all around him.

The shepherds, in defence of their flock, began to throw stones with their slings at the strange, furious figure. Just as Don Quixote was calling upon Alifanfaron to meet him in single combat, a large stone caught him on the side with such force that it broke two of his ribs and knocked the wind out of him. On the point of passing out, he remembered his balsam and pulled the flask and took a sip. But as he was doing so, another whizzing stone struck his raised hand, almost broke two of his fingers, smashed the flask to pieces and carried away

HE BEGAN SPEARING LAMBS AND SHEEP
ALL AROUND HIM.

three or four of his teeth. He fell from his horse stunned and the shepherds, believing they had killed him, whoever he was, gathered their sheep, collected the carcasses of those that had been killed and moved along as fast as they could.

Sancho Panza came running to the aid of his master, full of complaints and scolding him. "Did I not tell you they were only sheep and you had no reason to meddle with them?"

"Ah," exclaimed Don Quixote, "how easily that thief of an enchanter, my mortal enemy, can transform things or make them invisible. He envies the glory I would gain from battle so much that he transforms armies into flocks."

Seeing the state of his master's mouth, Sancho went back to his donkey to get something from the pouches to clean it with. It was then he discovered, to his sadness, that the bags were missing. In fact, the innkeeper had taken them as payment, though Sancho had not noticed the loss during his hasty exit from the inn. He vowed he would return home, abandoning his master and the wages he was owed, and his hopes of governing an island.

When Don Quixote heard of the loss, his dismay was nearly as great as his squire's. Now, to the immediate pangs of hunger, was added the prospect of starvation. But he did the best he could to cheer his man and they agreed their only course was to push on and find an inn where they could get food and lodging. "And pray to heaven," said Sancho, "that there will not be any blanket-tossers, or spirits, or enchanted **Moors** there."

Since they were on the high road they reasoned they must sooner or later come to an inn. But the way was long, they moved slowly, and night fell as they were still on the road.

Suddenly they saw a great number of moving lights coming in their direction. Presently they saw these were carried by a vast throng of figures, dressed in white, who carried a black **litter** in their midst.

Sancho immediately hid along the side of the road, but Don Quixote held his ground, determined to confront the spectral crowd.

"Ho! Knights," he shouted. "Halt! Whoever you are, tell me what you are carrying away, for either you are doing evil work or someone has done evil to you. In either case, I am here to punish or avenge you.

MOORS
Arabs who crossed from Africa and held Spain as a Muslim country from 731 to 1492. They are admired for their contributions to art, architecture, and higher learning.

LITTER
A covered and curtained couch on poles in which one person was carried.

One of the white figures in front, mounted on a mule, answered, "We are in haste, for the nearest inn is still a long way off and we have no time to stop and answer you."

"Stand!" said Don Quixote. "And treat me with civility. Tell me what I demand or prepare for battle."

As the man tried to push past him, Don Quixote grabbed the bridle of the mule, which immediately caused the mule to rear on its hind legs, and threw the rider over the horse's rear to the ground. Another man came forward and began to yell at Don Quixote for his violence. This was more than the knight could bear. He lowered his lance and charged the crowd. He drove one man to the ground and turned to attack the others, but they, a cowardly lot, scattered in all directions, looking, with their white robes and torches, like masqueraders after a carnival.

Don Quixote returned to the fallen man and, threatening him with his lance, demanded that he surrender.

"I am surrendered enough," the man said, "seeing as my leg is broken and I cannot move. I beg you not to harm me more. I am in **Holy Orders**. I and eleven other brothers have

HOLY ORDERS
In the Catholic Church, Brothers of the Dominican Order, which emphasizes preaching, wear white.

come from Baeza to escort that casket, which contains the body of a gentleman we are taking to Segovia, his birthplace, for burial."

"And who killed him?" asked Don Quixote.

"God, by a fever," answered the man.

"Then," said Don Quixote in a disappointed tone, "there is nothing for me to set right. You must know that I am Don Quixote de la Mancha, and it is my business to go about the world righting wrongs."

"Then I beg you, your worship," said the man, "right the wrong you have done to me by freeing my leg from under this mule."

"Why did you not say so before?" replied Don Quixote. "I might have gone on talking to you all night without finding out."

He called Sancho to come help him, but the sensible and hungry squire was just then ransacking a pack mule that belonged to the funeral procession. He had made his cloak into a sort of sack and was cramming it full with food.

When he was done and the bundle was tied safely to his own donkey, he responded to his master's call. Very soon they had freed the trapped man, mounted him on his mule, and putting a torch in his hand, sent him on to rejoin his companions.

Don Quixote wanted to stay to examine the casket, but Sancho persuaded him to leave at once so that they could find a peaceful place to eat the first food they had touched that day. They soon came to a secluded valley where they camped on fresh grass and made a hearty meal. But they found no wine among the monks' provisions, which greatly disappointed Sancho, and they did not even have water to wash down their food.

Noticing how green the grass was, however, they concluded they must be near a spring or brook and set out in search of it. Soon they heard the sound of falling waters and hurried in its direction. But as they went farther they also heard other sounds, heavy blows at regular intervals with the clanging of iron and rattling of chains. They stopped to listen, but could not understand the noise.

The hour was late and the night was pitch black. They were in the midst of lofty trees whose high leaves made strange whisperings. The place was solitary and mysterious. Filled now with fear, Sancho began trembling. But Don Quixote, mounted on Rocinante, took up his lance and shield and announced that he was going on to explore the haunted glen. He told Sancho to tighten the saddle and then gave him some final instructions.

"Wait here three days, and if at the end of that time I do not return, go home to our village and then to Toboso. Tell my Lady Dulcinea that her knight died attempting impossible deeds to make himself worthy of her."

Sancho, who was extremely afraid of being left in that diabolical place, cried when his master said these words. He tried to think of some way of diverting his master from his purpose. He begged him to return to the high road, even if they had to go three days without water. At any rate, there was no reason not to wait until morning to see first where they were. Don Quixote only answered that a knight-errant could not be troubled by darkness or supernatural sounds, nor should it ever be said of him, when dead or alive, that he had been turned from his duty by tears. So, frustrated in this attempt, Sancho decided on a more mechanical means.

Pretending to be busy with the saddle, he quietly tied the hind legs of the animal together, using the reins of his donkey, so that when Don Quixote wished to move forward, Rocinante could only manage a series of short jumps. Sancho said this was clear sign from heaven that the knight was to stay where he was until morning. Don Quixote, who had no better explanation for why Rocinante couldn't move, accepted this interpretation. He refused, however, to dismount to sleep. Sancho was ready to forget his troubles in slumber, but too frightened to lose sight of his master.

Since it seemed they would have to pass the night this way, Sancho proposed that he tell an entertaining story. Don Quixote cheerfully agreed. Holding tight to his master's saddle, while the eerie clanging went on steadily, Sancho began his tale.

"Once upon a time, he said, "there lived in Estramadura a goatherd named Lopes Ruiz, who fell in love with a shepherdess by the name of Torralva, who was the daughter of a rich herdsman, and this rich herdsman was—"

"If you go on this way, your story will take two days to listen to," said Don Quixote. "Tell it right off in a sensible way or drop it altogether."

"I am telling it just as I heard it, and as it is always told in my neighborhood, and I cannot tell it in another way, and it is not right for you to ask me to."

"Well, tell it as you please, but get on with it,"

"Well, then," said Sancho, "this Lopes Ruiz was in love with the shepherdess Torralva, who was a fine young woman, though she looked a little like a man, with a pair of small moustaches on her upper lip. And since they loved each other, and time went on, day following day, until the devil—who never rests, and is always watching to make trouble—took an interest in the two lovers, so that at last the shepherd lost all his love for the shepherdess and came to hate her as much as he had first loved her. Perhaps her desire to always make him jealous had something to do with it, but in any case he could no longer stand the sight of her and decided to leave the country altogether and go where he would never see her again. So he gathered his goats in one great flock and drove them west toward the frontier of Portugal, intending to stay in that kingdom. But Torralva, who really loved him all the time and did not want to lose him, followed after him, her legs naked, a staff in her hand, and a satchel around her neck, in which she carried her mirror and a comb and a small pot of makeup.

"The herdsman went on, followed by Torralva, until he came to the river **Guadiana**, which was in flood at the time and difficult to cross. He could see no boat or ferry to take him and his goats to the other side. This vexed him because he saw Torralva coming nearer and he did not want to be pestered with her tears. At last he found a fisherman with a small boat who could carry over one goat at a time, and, since he could do no better, he made a bargain with him to ferry his animals over.

GUADIANA
The river that forms part of the border between Portugal and Spain.

"The fisherman carried one goat over and left it. Then he came back and took over another goat and left it. Then he came back and took another goat over and left it—will your honor keep careful count of the goats as they are carried over?

It is of the greatest importance to the story that we make no mistake in the number as we go on.

"Then the fisherman took another goat over and left it, as I was saying. I should add that because the river was flooding, the banks were very muddy and slippery and that caused great trouble and delay. However, the fisherman came back and managed to get another goat over, then returned and got another, and then returned and got another."

"Why not assume that he got them all over at last?" asked Don Quixote. "With all this coming and going it will take a year to finish your story."

"How many have already crossed over, your honor?" asked Sancho.

"The devil knows!" said Don Quixote, "I don't!"

"There now!" said Sancho. "I asked your honor to keep careful count, and you have not, and the whole story is spoiled."

"How can that be?" asked Don Quixote. "What can it matter to the story to keep count of every single goat?"

"It matters because if I go wrong on the exact number, the rest of the story flies out of my head at once and I can't remember a word more."

"In that case the story is finished," said Don Quixote. "But I'm not surprised you have forgotten the rest of it. This infernal noise we have listened to all night is enough to distract anyone's mind."

As dawn now began to appear, Sancho thought it wise to untie Rocinante's feet. As soon as the poor beast found itself released, it began capering about. Don Quixote took this for a sign that he was now free to investigate the cause of the noise. So once more he said goodbye to Sancho and repeated his instructions about waiting three days. Sancho, however, intended to keep him in sight as long as he could and, taking his donkey's bridle, followed his master on foot.

They had not gone far through the trees when they came to a waterfall, with some decaying sheds nearby, and then they came in full view of the source of the strange noise. There were six huge **fulling hammers**, lifting and pounding in regular succession through the action of a waterwheel. Don Quixote was dumbfounded. Sancho, reacting to the fear he had felt, burst out laughing, which his master, in spite of his annoyance, could not help joining.

FULLING HAMMERS
Felt was made by pounding wet woolen cloth with massive wooden timbers for hours until the wool fibers became tightly matted together.

It had begun to rain and Sancho proposed that they go into the fulling mill for shelter, but Don Quixote was so disappointed with the whole affair that he refused to go nearer and led the way out of the wood and onto a road similar to the one they had traveled the day before.

Soon they perceived a man on horseback coming along with something on his head that shone like burnished gold.

"Here comes a knight on a gray charger," exclaimed Don Quixote, "who, if I am not mistaken, has on his head the famous golden helmet of Mambrino."

"All I see," said Sancho, "is a man on a gray donkey, like my Dapple, with something on his head that glistens."

"Exactly," said Don Quixote. "That is the helmet of Mambrino. Stand aside and see how, without a word, I shall secure the helmet."

"I shall certainly get out of the way," said Sancho, "and I hope this is not like the fulling mill affair."

"I forbid you ever to mention the fulling mill again," said his master in a rage. "If you do, I will mill your very soul for you."

Now the fact of the matter was this traveler was a barber who worked in two nearby villages, carrying with him his brass **basin** and other tools of his trade. When it had begun to rain, he had put the basin on his head to protect his new hat. As he came closer, Don Quixote spurred Rocinante and charged at him at a gallop, crying

BASIN
A barber's bowl had a circular notch cut in its rim so it could fit around a customer's neck.

out: "Defend yourself, coward, or surrender what is due to me!"

The astonished barber saw no way to avoid being run through with the lance than to slip off his donkey and dash away as fast as he could.

Don Quixote ordered Sancho to pick up the basin, which had fallen to the ground. Don Quixote took it from him and clapped it on his head, turning it around and around, trying to find the visor. "No doubt the pagan for whom this helmet was first made had an enormous head, and it is a pity the visor is missing." On hearing the basin described as a helmet, Sancho burst out laughing.

"What are you laughing at?" demanded Don Quixote sternly.

"I was only laughing, sir," said Sancho meekly, "at the idea of the enormous head the pagan must have had."

"I fancy," said Don Quixote, "that it must have fallen once into the hands of a greedy and ignorant person, who melted it down for its gold and then made this thing with what was left, which certainly does bear some resemblance to a barber's basin."

"And as for this charger," said Sancho, "which looks so much like a white donkey, what are we to do with it, for it seems the coward has abandoned it? And it is a better beast than my old Dapple."

"It is not customary to take a defeated knight's horse, unless the victor has lost his own in the combat," answered the knight. "Therefore, leave this animal and doubtless the owner will come back for it later."

"Can I at least trade equipment?" pleaded Sancho.

"I am not clear on that, but I know of nothing against such an exchange in the case of real necessity."

Sancho declared that no greater necessity could possibly exist and immediately traded his equipment for that on the white donkey, which was very much to his advantage.

CHAPTER 5

The Adventure with the Galley Slaves

W ITH ROCINANTE CHOOSING THE WAY, MASTER and man conversed as they went on, about knight-errants, heroic achievements, lovely princesses, kings and emperors, and so forth. Don Quixote talked in detail about the various methods and chances by which a knight's squire might make a rich marriage–though Sancho was already married–and acquire wealth, a title and status. They agreed that as soon as Don Quixote became king, he would make Sancho a duke. Meanwhile, they saw a curious sight on the road ahead of them.

It was a group, or line, of a dozen men on foot, strung together at the neck, like beads, by a heavy iron chain, and all handcuffed. With them were two men on horseback, with muskets, and two men on foot with pikes and swords. As soon as Sancho Panza saw them, he said, "This is a chain gang, impressed by the king, going to the **galleys**."

"How impressed?" said Don Quixote. "Is it possible that the king has the power to impress anyone he pleases?"

"I mean that those people, on account of their crimes, have been condemned by the king to serve in the galleys and are being taken to them by force," Sancho answered.

GALLEYS
Low ships moved by oars and sails that were often used in war.

"In effect, then, they are not going of their own free will," said Don Quixote.

"True," replied Sancho.

"In that case," said his master, "here is an occasion for me to perform my duty, which is to oppose violence and help those who are suffering."

"But, your worship," said Sancho, "the king, for the sake of justice, does no wrong or violence to such men, but only punishes them for their crimes."

By this time the chain gang had come up to them. Don Quixote, using many courteous phrases to the guards, asked why the men were being conducted so in chains.

One of the mounted guards replied that they were convicts, the King's slaves, who were going to the galleys, and there was no more to be said. The other mounted guard, who acted as their chief, said, "We have the official records of these wretches with us, but it is not a convenient time to read them."

"All the same," said Don Quixote, "I should like to know from each of them individually the cause of his misfortune."

"For falling in love," was the first man's answer.

"For no more than that!" exclaimed Don Quixote. "If one is to be sent to the galleys for that, I myself should be rowing there."

"But mine was not the sort of love your worship is thinking of," said the fellow. "It was a strong affection for a laundry basket of fine linen, which I embraced so ardently that it was only separated from me by the force of the law. I was caught in the act, so there was no need to torture me to confess. They gave my shoulders a hundred lashes and added three years in the galleys to finish the job."

Don Quixote similarly asked the second man, but he would not answer, being sad, so the first one answered for him.

"This man, sir, passes for a canary, in other words, a singer."

"Are singers sent to the galleys?" asked Don Quixote.

"I SHOULD LIKE TO KNOW FROM EACH OF THEM THE CAUSE OF
HIS MISFORTUNE," SAID DON QUIXOTE.

"Yes, sir," said the convict. "There is nothing worse than singing when you are in pain."

"I have always heard the saying, 'to sing in grief gives relief'," Don Quixote answered.

"In this case it is just the opposite," the convict said. "For he who sings once may have to weep the rest of his life."

"I do not understand."

But one of the guards explained. "You see, sir, among these rogues, singing in pain means to confess under torture. They tortured this man and he confessed to stealing cattle. So he was sentenced to six years in the galleys, plus two hundred lashes on his shoulders. He is always downcast because the others with him hate and abuse him because he confessed and had not the nerve to persist in denying his guilt. As they put it, 'No' is as easy to say as 'Yes.' They think a criminal has good luck when his fate depends only his own tongue and not on witnesses and evidence, and I imagine they are mostly right."

Don Quixote went on to the third convict.

This man told his story freely and carelessly. "I am going to the galleys for the want of ten **ducats**."

"I will give you twenty," said Don Quixote, "to relieve you from your present situation."

DUCATS
Gold
coins.

"If at the right time I had had the twenty ducats your lordship mentions," replied the convict, "I could have paid a smooth-talking lawyer, and today I would be standing free in the marketplace of Toledo, instead of traveling this road in a dog's leash. But, enough of this. God is great and I must be patient."

Don Quixote went on to the fourth man, who had a long, gray beard hanging down on his chest. He began to weep and said not a word. However, the man next to him said, "This fellow goes to the galleys for four years for selling women to men, witchcraft and fortune-telling."

The old man admitted his offenses, but said he meant no harm, and bemoaned the fact that at his age and in his state of health, he would never be free again. Sancho felt such compassion for the old man that he took a coin from his pocket and gave it to him in charity.

Don Quixote went on to the next man, who explained, with even more liveliness than the others, his tangled relations with girls. "The proofs are clear against me," he said. "And as I have no friends and no money, and my neck was about to be stretched, I am satisfied with the price of six years in the galleys. I am still young, and while there is life, there is hope." This man wore the clothes of a student, and one of the guards said he was a wonderful speaker.

Last of all came a fine-looking man of about thirty years of age, who was cross-eyed. He was chained hand and foot, and had an extra iron collar around his neck; his hands were manacled to an iron belt around his waist so that he could not raise them to his head or lower his head to reach his hands. Don Quixote inquired why this man was so specially guarded and one of the officers replied that it was because he was guilty of more crimes than all the rest put together and was such a desperate and violent ruffian that, despite how shackled he was, they always feared he would escape.

"What crimes has he committed that he deserves no more punishment than being sent to the galleys?" asked Don Quixote.

"He is going for ten years, which is like being con-demned to death," answered the guard. "This is no other than Gines de Pasamonte, alias Ginesillo de Parapilla. He has writ-ten a clever history of his own life and left the book in pawn at the prison for 200 reals."

Don Quixote asked if the book were finished.

"How can I finish it if I am still alive," answered the fellow himself. "So far, it relates everything about me, from my birth to this last time of being sent to the galleys."

"Then you have been sent before?"

"In the service of God and my country I have done four years before now, and I well know the taste of biscuits and the lash," replied Gines. "I am not much troubled about going again, as I shall have time to write and I have many more things to say. In the galleys of Spain there is leisure enough for my purpose."

"You seem clever," said Don Quixote.

"And unfortunate," answered Gines, "for misfortune always persecutes genius."

"Persecutes rascals, you mean," said the chief guard.

"Enough," said Gines. "Let's get on."

At this Don Quixote turned around to the chain gang and addressed them so: "From all you have told me, dear brothers, I gather that although you are being punished for your crimes, what you are going through is not to your taste and it is not with your good will that you are on your way to the galleys. It may be that this man's lack of endurance under torture, that man's lack of money, the other man's lack of influential friends, and the prejudiced views of your judges have been the causes of your condemnation and you have not had the full justice you are entitled to.

"All this is, to my mind, urging me, even forcing me, to make clear through you why Heaven has sent me into this world to be a professor of chivalry, which I am. I have sworn to help the wretched and defend those who are oppressed by the strong. But what can be done by fair means should not be done by force. I therefore beg these gentlemen who are guarding you to free you and let you depart in peace. There are many who would serve the king with a better will, and it does seem to me a hard case to make slaves of those whom God and nature made free.

"Besides, gentlemen," said Don Quixote to the guards, "these poor fellows have done you no wrong. We are all offenders here on earth and there is a God above who will punish the bad and reward the good. This is a reasonable request and I make it meekly and gently so that I can thank you for granting it, but if you will not do so, this lance and sword and my invincible arm will force you to."

"This is pleasant foolery," said the chief guard. "The silly mouse pops his head out of his hole at last! He wants us to release the prisoners of the king as if we had the authority to do so, or he had the power to command it. Go on your way in peace, sir. Pay attention to keeping your barber's bowl on top of your head and don't go looking for five legs on a cat."

"A mouse and a cat yourself," answered Don Quixote, and he immediately attacked the officer (who had no chance to defend himself) and drove him to the ground with a lance thrust that wounded him badly.

For a moment the other guards were stunned at the unexpected incident, but they soon advanced against Don Quixote, who calmly waited for their attack. No doubt it would have gone hard on him, but the convicts, seeing their chance to be free, began trying to break the chain that tied them together. This distracted the guards, who, trying to decide between engaging Don Quixote and controlling the prisoners, ended up doing nothing of use. Meanwhile, Sancho gave Gines de Pasamonte a hand at removing his shackles and he was the first in the gang to get free.

Gines at once threw himself on the wounded guard and seized his sword and pistol. He threatened the other guards with them, but held his fire, and they soon scurried away, both out of fear of Pasamonte's pistol and because of the stones thrown at them by the convicts.

Sancho wanted go at once to the nearby mountains, naturally fearing that the guards would raise a search after them, but Don Quixote would not leave before talking to the convicts, who by now had stripped the wounded guard naked. Calling them together, he reminded them of what he had done for them, and how much they owed him, and commanded them therefore to go to Toboso and there to lay the chain that had bound them together at the feet of Lady Dulcinea, and tell how they were freed by the heroic feats of Don Quixote. After that they could go where they pleased.

Gines de Pasamonte spoke for all the convicts, saying that they could not do any such thing now. Instead they must

HE COMMANDED THEM TO GO TO TOBOSO
AND TELL DULCINEA HOW THEY WERE FREED.

scatter and hide from the pursuit of justice. He proposed that
they should each say prayers for their rescuer, since they could
do this as they ran and hid.

This put Don Quixote in a rage and he demanded
that Pasamonte go himself and carry the chain on his back.

Pasamonte, seeing now the mental state of the man he
was dealing with, motioned to the convicts to step back a few
paces, where they began throwing a hurricane of stones at the

knight and his squire. Sancho tried to hide behind his donkey, but Don Quixote and Rocinante were exposed to the full force of the storm and in a short time both lay flat on the ground, very badly bruised. Pasamonte then ruthlessly attacked Don Quixote, beating him with the brass barber's basin repeatedly and then banging the basin on the ground until it was almost smashed in pieces. Next they stripped off his jacket and trousers. Sancho's cloak was taken too, and, after hurriedly dividing the spoils, they made off in different directions and were quickly out of sight.

CHAPTER 6

Flight into the Mountains and Sancho's Errand

A S SOON AS DON QUIXOTE AND SANCHO WERE ABLE TO take the road again, they made for the mountains to hide for a time, talking as they went about the ingratitude of some people. By night time they arrived at the gorges of the Sierra Morena, and after searching a little, they selected a resting place between two rocks in a grove of **cork trees**. But fate had it that the villain Pasamonte wandered in the same direction and arrived at the very spot where master and

CORK TREES
A type of oak tree native to the Mediterranean whose light, waterproof bark is stripped off about every ten years to make such things as bottle stoppers.

man, worn out with the sufferings of the day, had fallen into a deep sleep. Pasamonte recognized them, and seeing how soundly they slept, cast covetous eyes on the knight's horse and the squire's donkey. The horse he judged to be of little use and no cash value, but the donkey was sturdy.

But taking it was no easy matter, for Sancho, anxious over the safety of his cherished Dapple in that wild country, where robbers might prowl at night, had arranged himself to sleep as best he could on the back of his beast. Crouched on his wooden saddle, Sancho slept as if he was in a feather bed, and in that state Pasamonte studied him as he thought of his plan. After a while, he cut four stakes of wood and quietly propped them under the four corners of the saddle. Then, gently loosening the saddle, he led the donkey out from under it and made off with the beast, leaving Sancho still mounted and undisturbed.

At the break of day Sancho awoke, yawned and stretched, and instantly fell to the ground in a heap. He looked around in amazement to see what had happened and where Dapple was, but by that time she was many miles away. Sancho realized the trick that had been played on him and the loss he had suffered. He let go of his feelings so vociferously that the rocks all around echoed with his wailing. His uproar awoke Don Quixote, who saw what was wrong and tried to

HE MADE OFF WITH THE BEAST, LEAVING SANCHO
STILL MOUNTED AND UNDISTURBED.

comfort his grieving squire. Sancho at last calmed down after Don Quixote promised him three of the donkeys he had at home.

After eating what was left of their food for breakfast, the knight and squire resumed their aimless wanderings through the glens and ravines of the country. Presently they came upon what appeared to be signs that some unfortunate traveller had lost his way, and probably his life, in the wilderness. First they found a saddle cushion with a leather case strapped to it, both so rotten they must have been lying there abandoned for a long time. The case contained linen underwear, a pocket-book and more than a hundred gold coins. In the pocket book were some sad love poems, which Don Quixote read with deep interest and sympathy. Sancho, meanwhile (with the permission of his master), stuffed the money in a pouch and thought he was richly rewarded for all he had gone through. Later on they came upon the carcass of a mule lying in a creek, still saddled, but half devoured by birds and beasts of prey.

An old goatherd they met later was able to throw some light on the mystery. According to him, the traveller was indeed a lovesick shepherd who had wandered into those parts and gone stark mad. He was still haunting the mountains, running around almost naked and at times very dangerous to

LATER THEY CAME UPON THE CARCASS OF A MULE.

solitary people he met. Don Quixote resolved to see him if he could, and during his stay in the mountains he did come across him twice, but to no purpose. The madman, in his more normal moments, would tell Don Quixote long tales of his romantic troubles, and then his fury would break out fresh, to the danger of those near.

It was, perhaps, the spectacle of this unhappy being and the loneliness of the surroundings that inspired Don Quixote with a new idea. He remembered that Amadis of Gaul once, in a similar wilderness, had decided to go mad and act out his desperate love for Angelica the Fair, who had rejected him, in order to prove the depth of his affection for her. He had stripped naked and run about tearing up rocks and trees, and doing a thousand other things worthy of eternal fame. Don Quixote decided to imitate his example and told his intention to Sancho.

"But, sir," said Sancho, "what cause have you to go mad? Lady Dulcinea has not disdained you, or preferred someone else."

"That is the point," answered the knight. "There is nothing much in a knight-errant going mad for a good reason. The thing is to do it for no reason whatever. Besides, my long absence from Lady Dulcinea is cause enough. I will go mad until you have taken a letter from me to her and returned with an answer."

IN HIS MORE NORMAL MOMENTS, HE WOULD TELL
DON QUIXOTE OF HIS ROMANTIC TROUBLES.

"Dear God!" said Sancho earnestly. "In some matters
I cannot understand your worship, for you say and do things
that make me think knight-errantry is mostly make-believe
and that you know it."

"Is it possible that you have been with me all this time
without being sure of that?" said Don Quixote. "Of course the
affairs of knights are mostly delusions, simply because of the

many wicked sorcerers who transform everything in order to frustrate and mislead us. We can see things like windmills and barber's basins as plainly as others, but we can also see that they can be disguises for giants or magic helmets."

As they talked they came to the foot of a rugged mountain with a green and pleasant valley on the side of it, through which a small creek ran. This Don Quixote declared to be the place where he would stay, alone and naked, while Sancho went on his errand to the Princess of Toboso. Sancho suggested using Rocinante to speed his journey, and Don Quixote agreed. However, he desired that Sancho not leave at once, but wait and witness him tearing up his clothes, throwing his arms around wildly, knocking his head against rocks, and other acts suggesting insanity.

"For the love of heaven," Sancho said, "be careful how you trifle with your head, sir, for you might happen to hit it against a sharp point of rock and put an end to yourself. If your worship thinks something of the kind must be done, why not ram your head against water, or something soft like cotton and let me report what I please to Lady Dulcinea? What does it matter, seeing that it is all make-believe?"

"No," said Don Quixote. "My madness must be no mere mockery. But you can leave me some lint and ointment to dress my wounds while you are away."

"If your worship will write the letter at once," Sancho replied. "I will hasten off with it and return without delay to take care of you."

Don Quixote wrote out the letter on a sheet of paper taken from the pocketbook and told Sancho to have it recopied in good handwriting before he gave it to Lady Dulcinea.

"She does not know my handwriting, so it will not matter," he said. "Indeed, during the twelve years I have been in love with her I have only seen her three times, and she has never bothered to cast her eyes on me, such is the seclusion she is kept in by her father, Lorenzo Corchuelo."

"What!" exclaimed the squire. "The daughter of Lorenzo Corchuelo, who is named Aldonza, is the Lady Dulcinea del Toboso?"

"It is she," answered Don Quixote.

"Why, I know her very well," said Sancho. "And fine strapping girl she is, too. She can lift as much as the strongest man in the parish and I bet she could hold her own against any knight that has ever ridden a horse. And what a splendid voice she has. I remember one day she climbed the church tower to call to laborers in the fields and was heard a mile away as if she was standing beside them. And what courage! She makes a game of everybody and never fails to pay back a joker, with

DON QUIXOTE WROTE THE LETTER
AND THEN READ IT ALOUD.

interest. But what is the good of sending vanquished knights to her. When they find her threshing in the barn or working in the fields, and fall on their knees before her, she may only laugh at them or think they are making fun of her, which might be worse for them."

"Friend Sancho," said Don Quixote, "you are an eternal babbler and you lack understanding, as I have told you before. The lady in question serves my purpose admirably. Do you think, you ignorant, foolish man, that the famous ladies in books and ballads are really ladies of flesh and blood? Certainly not, they are mostly imaginary persons. It is enough for me if I imagine Aldonza to be the most beautiful, most gracious princess in the world."

THEN HE TORE OFF HIS CLOTHES, DANCED
IN THE AIR, AND TUMBLED OVER A FEW TIMES.

"Your worship is always right and I am a mere fool," answered Sancho. "Let me have the letter and be on my way."

Don Quixote wrote the letter and then read it aloud to Sancho so that if by any chance it was lost he would know its general message. This was the letter:

"High and Sovereign Lady!–

He who is stabbed by the point of absence and pierced by arrows of love, O sweet Dulcinea del Toboso, greets thee with wishes for that health which he does not enjoy himself. If your beauty despises me, if you favor me not, and if your disdain still follows me, though I am used to suffering, I can hardly endure a sickness so severe and so lasting. My good squire Sancho will tell you, O fair beloved one, of the condition I am reduced to on your account. If it is your pleasure to accept me, I am yours. If not, do what seems good to you, for my death will only mean the end of your cruelty and my own passion. Yours until death–

The Knight of the Sorrowful Face"

Sancho said how magnificent a composition it was and then mounted Rocinante and prepared to ride away. But Don Quixote ordered him to stay and watch some mad tricks. Don Quixote then tore off his clothes, danced in the air and tumbled himself over a few times, so that when Sancho left he felt he could honestly swear that his master was crazy.

CHAPTER 7

Conspiracy,
Recovery of Dapple,
Slaying a Giant,
and Home Again

S ANCHO TOOK THE HIGH ROAD FOR TOBOSO. THE NEXT
day he sighted the inn where they had tossed him in a
blanket and as he looked at it, fearfully, he saw two men
come out whom he recognized at once as the priest and the
barber from his native village. These two friends of Don
Quixote were in fact searching for the poor gentleman and
when they saw Sancho they demanded an account of his master, whose horse he was riding. After hesitating, Sancho told

SANCHO FOUND HIM AT LAST IN A ROCKY RECESS.

them the whole story of their adventures, where his master was, and what he was about.

That night they remained at the inn and considered the best means of getting the knight back to his house. They came to the conclusion that the most promising plan was to lure him away by pretending that the Lady Dulcinea had commanded his presence at Toboso. They instructed Sancho carefully in the part he was to play in carrying it out.

On the following day, Sancho started off to return to his knight. The priest and the barber would follow at a more leisurely pace. Once in the mountains, the squire hunted for his master and found him at last in a rocky recess, with clothes on and his armor hanging from the branch of a tree. The knight was surprised to see him so soon, but immediately began asking him questions about his mission to Dulcinea.

Sancho's powers of invention were severely strained, but he had a good deal of natural ingenuity and had been well coached by the priest and barber in what to say. He said at once, truthfully, that in his haste to leave he had forgotten the letter Don Quixote had written to Dulcinea. And indeed, two days after he left, the knight had found the letter still in the pocketbook. Sancho said that because he remembered the message so well he had not returned for the letter. The rest of his story had nothing to do with the truth. He told his master, "I repeated the contents of the letter to a parish clerk in a place I came to, and he wrote it down, and I took it on to Toboso."

"No doubt you found my Queen of Beauty in a stately apartment stringing pearls on gold thread," said Don Quixote.

"No, sir," replied Sancho. "I found her **winnowing** bushels of wheat in her father's backyard. When I offered her the letter she told me to put it down until her hands were free. While I waited I helped her move sacks."

WINNOWING
Separating kernels of wheat from their shells, called chaff, by tossing it in the air and allowing the wind to blow the chaff away.

"Then surely you perceived a fragrance, a perfume like that of a fancy shop," said Don Quixote.

"Well," said the squire, "she smelled pretty strong. I thought it was garlic and onions, but she was sweating hard from the work so it's hard to know. When she stopped working she picked up the letter and ripped it up, for she can neither read nor write and did not want her secret to become known by asking anybody to read the letter to her. So I told her all about your worship's love for her and she said she would a thousand times rather see you than read the letter. You are to leave off your pranks among the rocks and briars. And I asked her if a Biscayan fellow had come to her and she said one had, but she knew nothing of Gines de Pasamonte or the galley slaves."

"I suppose she gave you a jewel when you departed?"

"All she gave me was a piece of bread and cheese," he answered.

"I go to her at once in obedience to her command," said Don Quixote, which was just what Sancho wanted to hear. "There is only one thing I do not understand. It is more than thirty **leagues** from here to Toboso, yet you have only been journeying three days to there and back."

LEAGUE
A league is a measure of distance that ranges from 2.5 to 4 miles.

"I cannot understand it myself," said Sancho, blushing. "I think there must be magic in it. Rocinante flew like the wind."

THE FAT SQUIRE UNHAPPILY TRUDGED ALONG ON FOOT.

"That is it," said Don Quixote. "It often happens that a friendly magician will enable a knight to get over a thousand leagues in a day."

While the knight, mounted on Rocinante, went on talking about this subject and the fat squire unhappily trudged alongside on foot, they came upon the priest and the barber pretending to be travellers at rest on the roadside. Sancho had been looking for them anxiously and was glad now to be free from the responsibility of telling more lies.

Don Quixote recognized them at once and got down to greet them. In answer to his inquiries about what brought them there, the priest said, "Our friend master Nicholas, the barber, and I were going to Seville to get an inheritance of sixty thousand crowns left to me by a relative of mine in India. But yesterday we were attacked by four highwaymen, who stripped us of everything worth taking. The thieves were said to be part of a gang of galley slaves set free in this region by a man valiant enough to overcome their guards, and mad enough to let loose such a pack of wolves."

Don Quixote hung down his head at these words, but Sancho cried out, "In truth, your reverence, it was my master who did that job."

"And if I did," said Don Quixote angrily, "it is because it is a knight's duty to help the distressed and suffering and I am prepared to make good this principle against anyone with my spear and sword."

No one present would accept the challenge and so they walked on in silence, until a very curious incident occurred. Sancho was plodding along wearily, full of regrets over his lost Dapple, when they saw a man on a gray donkey coming towards them. A single glance convinced Sancho that the man was riding the donkey he had just been thinking about, and a second look equally satisfied him that the rider was no other than the bandit Gines de Pasamonte disguised as a gypsy. The thief was just as quick to perceive the danger he had unexpectedly fallen into, and he jumped down and ran off at a speed that made pursuit hopeless.

Sancho ran to Dapple and, with many endearing words, kissed her and hugged her neck as if she had been a lost child. Mounted on her again, Sancho felt a new joy in life and thought no more of his recent troubles and discomforts.

Late in the afternoon of the next day the party reached the inn where the blanket-tossing incident occurred. Little was said of that topic after the innkeeper was assured that all charges would be paid this time. Don Quixote retired early, being overly fatigued, and soon fell into a feverish sleep. But the rest of the party, as well as other guests, stayed up very late talking and telling stories.

They were nearly finished when Sancho burst in among them and cried out with great dismay, "Come quickly to my master! He is in a desperate battle with an enormous giant, whose head he has sheared off his shoulders as clean as a turnip and blood is running everywhere."

They could now hear Don Quixote shouting, "Stand to it, scoundrel! You cannot escape me and your **scimitar** will not save you!" Then came the sound of blows against the walls.

"Bless me," said the innkeeper, "I hope your master has not interfered with the wine-bags hanging near his bed." And with that the whole company made for the knight's room.

SCIMITAR
A saber with a curved blade, mainly used by the Turks and Arabs.

The first thing they saw was Don Quixote standing in his shirt, with a little red nightcap on his head and a blanket over his left arm, slashing with his sword all around him. The landlord's fears proved true. The room was flooded with wine from the gashed wine-bags. The landlord lunged for Don Quixote, who seemed to be sleepwalking, but others kept him from harming the knight. The barber threw a bucket of water on Don Quixote to awaken him, but it hardly seemed to bring him to his senses.

Sancho declared that he had seen the giant and went looking for its head. Not finding it, he said the inn was enchanted.

"Why, you enemy of God and all the saints," said the landlord, "can't you see this is nothing but wine from those ripped-up skins? Neither you nor your crazy master will escape this time without paying every penny of the damages."

DON QUIXOTE WAS SLASHING WITH HIS SWORD
ALL AROUND HIM.

The priest calmed the innkeeper and his family down, promising that all the wines and skins would be paid for. Don Quixote, who still was in a state of fever, was put back to bed under Sancho's care and peace ruled the inn again.

It was several days before the knight was well enough to resume the homeward journey again, which he now made stretched out in a ox cart hired for that purpose. It was noon on Sunday when the party reached the village and everybody, especially the niece and housekeeper, was shocked to see how pale and thin and weak the knight was.

While he was being carried into the house to be put to bed, Sancho's wife Teresa came out to greet him. First she asked about Dapple's health and satisfied herself by looking over the donkey. Then she turned to her husband and asked him what profit he had to show for deserting his family. Her ruffled temper was smoothed however when she learned that he had come home with a hundred gold crowns, plus the wages he earned from the trip. As for the glory he claimed from it, she thought as little of that as she did of the prospect of being the governor of an island.

Many days later, when Don Quixote's health was improved and he and Sancho had been talking together, Sancho came home in such a cheery mood that his wife asked, "What makes you so pleased?"

"Wife of mine," he answered, "I am so well pleased that I would be more pleased if it pleased God that I was less pleased than I am pleased."

"I do not understand you, husband. How can one be pleased not to be pleased?"

"This way, Teresa: I am pleased to return to the service of Don Quixote, my master, who desires to go on adventures for a third time. I wish to come across another hundred crowns, if possible. I am sorry to part from you and the children, for if I could live at home at ease it would be better than tramping around on rough roads and that is why I say I would be better pleased, if God pleased that I was not so pleased to go."

"Look here, Sancho," said Teresa, "Ever since you went knight-erranting you talk in such a roundabout way that nobody can understand you."

"It is enough that God understands me. Take special care now of Dapple and see that she is in good condition and the pack saddle is in good order, for we shall have to endure many hardships, many giants and dragons and evil spirits, and hissings and roarings and bellowings and bleatings, not to mention enchanted Moors, who are worse than all the rest together. My only hope is for an island where I can live without trouble or danger."

"Why can't you do without an island?" said Teresa. "I don't understand you. Do what you please and don't bother me with your speeches. But if you are determined to be a governor, why not take your son Sancho with you and bring him up to the business."

"I will send for him, with plenty of money for his expenses, and as for our daughter Mary Sancho, she shall be a countess."

"Send money for the boy, but as for Mary, I shall think of her as being as good as dead the day she becomes a countess. But, do what you please, for wives must obey their husbands, even when they are blockheads."

On that parting shot, Sancho returned to his master, who was just then talking earnestly with Sampson Carrasco, a young friend and neighbor of Don Quixote who had recently finished his studies at the University of Salamanca. The young man was telling Don Quixote that his fame had spread far and wide and, in turn, listening to his views on knight-errantry, all with the idea of weaning Don Quixote from his delusions, or at least keeping him safe at home. He could think of no better treatment than one based on the very folly of the knight, and so, far from opposing the plan for a new expedition, he was encouraging it. His advice was a surprise to the knight and more so to the niece and housekeeper, who had supposed Carrasco would do his best to oppose the madness of their master. Three days later, however, Don Quixote and Sancho sallied forth again, the knight with a new helmet supplied by Carrasco, who insisted on escorting them well beyond the village.

CHAPTER 8

The Search for Dulcinea, Her Transformation, and the Masked Players

THE KNIGHT ON HIS BRAVE ROCINANTE AND SANCHO on his trusty Dapple, with pouches well-supplied and their purses full of money, set their course for Toboso, the home of the imaginary Lady Dulcinea, "for," said Don Quixote, "I must have all the blessings of her ladyship in order to have good fortune in the perilous adventures that await us."

"That may be," answered Sancho, "but it will be difficult to see her alone, or get her blessing, unless she tosses it over the fence of the yard where I saw her last time."

"You thought it was a fence? Impossible! You mean the galleries, the arcades of a rich and royal palace."

"All I can say," replied Sancho, "is that what I saw was a fence, if my eyesight and memory are worth anything."

"Well," said Don Quixote, "we shall go there, for whether there be chinks or lattices, one flash from the bright sun of her beauty will inflame my soul and fortify my heart so that no one will be able to compete with me in skill or courage."

"I did not see any flashes," said Sancho. "But that might be because the dust of the winnowing made a cloud around her face."

The next day they came in sight of Toboso without meeting any adventure. Deciding not to enter the town before nightfall, they rested in the shade of some oak trees near the road. It was much later when they got into the city and all the inhabitants seemed to be in bed; except for the barking of dogs, the whole town was hushed in silence.

"Lead on to the palace," said Don Quixote, "for it is possible she is still awake."

"What palace?" asked Sancho. "It was a small, ordinary house when I saw it."

"That was no doubt some pavilion attached to the castle, where the great ladies retire for amusement," said the knight.

"Well," said Sancho, "this is not the time to be rousing people from their beds, anyhow."

"First let's find the castle and then we'll decide what to do. See yonder, Sancho, that vast building must be my lady's palace."

"That is clearly a church," said Sancho, "and I have already told your worship that the lady lives down an alley."

"Blockhead!" cried the knight. "Do palaces exist on alleys?"

"I know not," answered Sancho. "Every country has its own customs and it may be the fashion here to build palaces on alleys and backyards."

They asked a passing laborer about Lady Dulcinea, but he knew nothing and, as day was beginning to break, Sancho suggested that they retire into some woods near town to rest. Later on he would come alone and search for her ladyship's house. The knight agreed and they rode a couple of miles out of town, where they found shelter in a shady grove.

It was still early in the day when Sancho emerged from the grove, pretending to go find Dulcinea and puzzled about how he would get around his master on this matter. He went a little way and then turned off the road, intending to hide until evening, so that Don Quixote would think he was occupied with his mission into Toboso.

He sat and thought for a long time and had not come to any conclusion, when, just as he was about to return to his master, he saw three peasant girls mounted on donkeys coming from the direction of the city. He had been thinking if only he could get a hold of some country girl, he could persuade his master that she was Lady Dulcinea in disguise, and here came the very thing he wanted. So, riding back to where Don Quixote sat, he called out:

"Mount at once, your worship, and ride into the road, for here comes Lady Dulcinea and two of her damsels to pay you a visit."

"Gracious Heaven!" exclaimed Don Quixote. "What do you say? You are not deceived, or are you deceiving me?"

"Not a bit," answered Sancho. "See for yourself. The princess and her attendants are blazing all over with gold and diamonds and pearls and rubies, and their hair flies behind their shoulders like bundles of sunbeams and they are mounted on the three finest belfrys you ever saw."

"You mean **palfreys**, Sancho."

"Belfrys or palfreys, it's all the same for what it matters. There they are at any rate–the finest ladies you ever set eyes on, especially Princess Dulcinea, who is perfectly dazzling."

As Sancho and Don Quixote emerged from the wood, Sancho whispered, "There they are, shining like the sun."

"I see only three plain-looking country girls," said Don Quixote, "riding on donkeys."

PALFREY
A light saddle horse suitable for a woman to ride.

"God save us!" said Sancho, pretending to be amazed. "Is it possible you see only donkeys where there are three belfrys, or whatever you call them, as white as pure snow?"

"I tell you, Sancho, they are donkeys–at least they appear so to me."

"Sir," said Sancho, solemnly, "say no more, but clear your eyes if you can and come pay reverence to the mistress of your soul, even if she be in a disguise."

Then he led the way to where the girls were passing, took hold of the bridle of one donkey, and fell to his knees in the dust, saying to the girl, "Queen, Princess, Duchess of Beauty, let your grandness be pleased to receive the homage of yon captive knight, who stands there turned to stone by your amazing beauty and magnificent presence. I am Sancho Panza,

SANCHO TOOK HOLD OF THE DONKEY'S BRIDLE
AND FELL TO HIS KNEES.

his squire, and he is Don Quixote de la Mancha, otherwise
known as the Knight of the Sorrowful Face."

By this time Don Quixote was also on his knees in
front of the girl, but he could see only her wide, homely face
and flat nose, and felt so confused he could not say a word.

For their part, the girls were astonished and bewildered both at being stopped and at being addressed in such a
fashion. The one who had been called "Queen" first broke the

silence, saying, "Get out of the way, you couple of fools, and let us go about our business."

"Oh, Princess and universal lady of Toboso," Sancho began, but stopped when another girl blurted out, "Shut up, you idiot! Go on your way! A pretty thing it is that three poor girls can't go along a public road without nincompoops like you and that other fellow trying to make fun of them."

"Rise, Sancho," whispered Don Quixote sadly. "I see now that fate has shot her last cruel arrow into my wretched heart. The enchanters have doomed me never to see, in her own person, the matchless Lady Dulcinea. Indeed, they have degraded her beauty into the coarse looks of a country girl and may even turn her into a goblin just to increase my suffering.

"Nevertheless," he said, turning to one of the girls, "be so good as to bestow on me one loving look, one kind word."

"Oh, bother," said the girl. "Talk your gibberish somewhere else. Leave us alone." They put their donkeys in motion and trotted quickly away. But they had not got far when the donkey of the one Don Quixote had imagined to be Lady Dulcinea began to kick and buck so that the girl was thrown to the ground. Sancho and Don Quixote ran to help her, but she was on her legs before they could do much. She ran toward her donkey, whose back was to her, vaulted into the saddle like a man and rode off laughing with her companions.

"By **St. Roque!**" exclaimed Sancho, "Our Lady Dulcinea is as agile as a bird and fit to ride against any jockey in Spain or Mexico."

Don Quixote watched the retreating figure and said sadly, "You see now, Sancho, how I am persecuted. The evil enchanters will not let me have the pleasure of seeing my lady as she really is. And they make her condition as unattractive to me as possible, for instead of the fragrant scent she has from living among flowers, they give her the smell of garlic, which I distinctly noticed."

ST. ROQUE

(Also Roch) A saint, born in France, who gave to the poor the vast riches he inherited and then travelled the roads in a pilgrim's garb. He went from city to city in Italy nursing victims of the plague, which he was thought to be able to cure through prayer. He survived the plague himself. In art, he is usually shown lifting away part of his clothing to show a plague sore. He was not recognized by his relatives when he returned home and his uncle, a judge, suspecting he was a spy, sent him to prison. There, forgotten for five years, he died. Thus did his family finally discover his identity. He is a patron saint of prisoners and the sick.

"They are vile creatures," agreed Sancho, "and I should like to see them all strung up by the gills like smoked fish. They might at least have left her breath alone, but I must say, all the same, that she seemed to me all sweetness and beauty, and she had on her lip a lovely mole with seven or eight splendid hairs growing out of it like threads of gold."

"Rather long hairs for a mole," said Don Quixote.

"Oh, I assure you they were there," answered Sancho.

"No doubt," said Don Quixote, "and if she had a hundred, they would all be additions to her beauty, like so many bright stars. But woe is me who is unable to see any of this. Surely I am the most unfortunate of men."

Sancho struggled to keep from laughing at the success of his trick. After some more conversation of the same sort, they mounted their beasts and took the road to Saragossa, where a great annual festival was about to take place.

CHAPTER 9

The Strange Knight and Squire– Challenge, Victory and Transformation

MASTER AND MAN LAID THEMSELVES DOWN TO PASS the night under some wide-spreading oak trees. Sancho slept soundly, but before long Don Quixote's lighter slumber was disturbed by the sound of voices. Sitting up, he saw two men on horseback and heard one say to the other, "Stop and attend to the horses, for this place seems to offer not only pasture, but the silence and solitude my thoughts of love require." With that the speaker dismounted and stretched out on the grass with such rattling of armor that

Don Quixote thought the man must be a knight-errant like himself. So he crept over to Sancho and whispered, "Wake up, Sancho, here is an adventure."

"I pray to heaven it will be a safe and profitable one," answered the drowsy squire.

Don Quixote explained what he had seen and heard, and just then the sound of a guitar reached them. "It certainly must be some knight or other in love," said Sancho.

"All knight-errants are in love," said Don Quixote. Then the mysterious knight began singing a love song—not very well, nor was his guitar-playing good. When he finished he sighed deeply and said, "Oh, most beautiful and cruel of women, divine Casildea de Vandalia, is your tormented knight to waste away in wandering and toil? Is it not enough that I have caused your superior beauty to be admitted by all the knights of Navarre, Leon, Castile, and all the knights of La Mancha?"

"That," said Don Quixote to Sancho, "is not true, for I am a knight of La Mancha and I have never made such an acknowledgement, nor will I ever make one so unfavorable to my lady. He is raving."

The strange knight, hearing voices, called out, "Who is there? Are you among the happy or the sad?"

"The sad," answered Don Quixote.

THE STRANGER'S SQUIRE DREW SANCHO ASIDE.

"Come here, then," said the stranger, "and behold the very model of sorrow and misery."

The mournful stranger took Don Quixote by the arm and invited him to sit down. "From what I have just heard from you," said Don Quixote, "I take it your woes are due to love–an unrequited passion for a fair lady?" The stranger nodded, and asked if Don Quixote was also suffering so.

"That is my fate," he replied, "though I cannot exactly say my lady scorns me."

"Certainly not," said Sancho, "for she is as gentle as a lamb and as soft as butter."

"Is this your squire?" demanded the stranger. "And do you allow him to speak when you are in a conversation?"

"I can talk and I have talked to better people than you. But never mind—the less said, the sooner mended," said Sancho.

The stranger's squire now drew Sancho aside, saying, "Come, let's chat together, and let our masters talk as they please about their love problems." And away they went to discuss the hardships squires put up with.

"The hope of reward," said the stranger's squire, "makes up for a lot. It is a poor knight-errant who cannot bestow an earldom, or a government, on his squire."

"Yes," answered Sancho, "my master has promised me the governorship of an island."

"Mine is offering me a fat **canonry.**"

CANONRY
A priest on the staff of a cathedral or in a religious community.

"Ah, then your master is a knight of the church, in some sort," said Sancho. "Mine was advised to be an **archbishop**, but he would be nothing less than the emperor. I am always afraid he will turn to the church and leave me in the lurch, for I have no learning that way."

"You may find," said the
other, "that island government is
more trouble than profit.
Likely enough, if we were wise
men we would stay at home
with our families instead of
tramping around the country
with a master like mine, who is as
crazy as he is brave, and even more
than that, is a scoundrel."

ARCHBISHOP
The head of a
province in the
Roman Catholic
Church.

"Mine is certainly mad," said Sancho,
"but he is not a liar. He's as honest and innocent as a babe. You
can persuade him of anything, and that is why I love him and
cannot leave him in spite of all his follies."

"It's the blind leading the blind," said the other, "and
we'll all end up in a ditch. But talking is making me dry. I have
something in my saddlebag that will moisten our tongues." As
he said it, he pulled out a flask of wine and a large rabbit pie
and both men went on eating, drinking, and talking until at
last they fell asleep.

Meanwhile their masters spent the time in courteous
knightly conversation. "Finally, sir," the other knight was saying, "I fell desperately in love with Casildea de Vandalia and
she tested my devotion by laying on me such tasks as those

imposed on **Hercules** by his step-
mother. One time she ordered
me to challenge the famous
giant-woman of Seville,
commonly called La
Giralda, who is as stout and
strong as brass, and who,
without moving from where
she is, is the most changeable
and fickle woman in the
world. **I came, I saw, I
conquered.** I made her stay
still for a week, even though
the wind blew constantly. I
was next commanded to
weigh the great antique **bulls of
Guisando**, a task more fitting to porters
than to a knight-errant. Another time she required me to
plunge into the abyss of **Cabra** and tell her what was
there. I have done all these things and
still my hopes are unfulfilled. Her disdain continues and her tyrannical com-
mands go on. Now she has ordered me to
cross all the provinces of Spain and force every knight-errant I

HERCULES
Hercules was the most popular of the ancient Greek heroes. He was a son of Zeus, the foremost of the Gods, and his mother was a mortal. Zeus' wife Hera therefore hated Hercules and drove him insane. While mad, Hercules killed his wife and children. When he recovered his sanity, he performed 12 feats, called his labors, to atone for his crime. All the tasks were thought to be impossible, among them killing the nine-headed Hydra and getting the golden apples of Hesperides, for which he lifted the world off Atlas' shoulders.

BULLS OF GUISANDO
Ancient carved figures near the city of Avila.

CABRA
A deep cave in the province of Cordoba.

meet to confess that she is the best and most beautiful of women and I am the bravest and most adoring knight in the world. I have crossed Spain from end to end and defeated all the knights who dared to oppose me, especially that famous one Don Quixote de la Mancha, who I compelled to confess that my Casildea is more beautiful than his Dulcinea. I consider my conquest of him to be equal to the defeat of all the knights of the world because he has defeated them all, and I therefore reap all his glory and fame."

I CAME, I SAW, I CONQUERED. A famous quote from Roman emperor Julius Caesar, who said it to explain the ease of one of his victories in battle. In Latin the phrase is "Veni, vidi, vici."

"Sir knight," said Don Quixote quietly, "I say nothing about your other victories, but I do not admit that you have vanquished Don Quixote de la Mancha. You may have overcome someone resembling him, but certainly not the man himself."

"How not the man himself?" exclaimed the knight of the wood. "I swear to you the contrary. Is he not tall, with a long, lean face and a hooked nose bent to one side, gray-haired, lanky-limbed, with a heavy, drooping mustache, and calls himself the Knight of the Sad Face or the Sorrowful Countenance? Moreover, he has for his squire a peasant by the name of Sancho, and for his horse a steed named Rocinante, and for his lady-love Dulcinea del Toboso, sometimes called

Aldonza Lorenzo. And if that is not enough to prove I am telling the truth, then here is my sword, which will force belief on the most incredulous."

"Softly, good sir. Listen to me for a moment," answered Don Quixote. "The man you speak of is a particular friend of mine, and though your description is fairly accurate on the whole, I am certain he is not the man in question. He has many enemies among the enchanters, one in particular, and one of these may have impersonated him and allowed himself to be defeated by you in order to damage Don Quixote's reputation. I can tell you as a fact that in the last couple of days evil enchanters have transformed the lovely Dulcinea del Toboso into a lowly peasant girl. And if you are still dissatisfied with what I say, then here stands, in person, Don Quixote himself, ready to prove his identity with his weapons in whatever fashion you prefer." Saying this, Don Quixote stood up, clutched the hilt of his sword, and waited for the knight to make his decision.

The strange knight replied quietly, "It is not becoming for knight-errants to perform feats of arms in the dark, like highwaymen," he said. "Let us wait for daylight, and let the conditions of battle be that the defeated shall obey the command of the victor, so long as the command is something a knight can obey without dishonoring himself."

Don Quixote agreed to this, and the two knights went to rouse their squires and order them to prepare for the looming combat.

The stranger's squire took the matter coolly enough. But Sancho was terribly frightened for his master, and even more for himself, because the other squire informed him that in this part of Spain it was customary for the squires of combating knights to fight each other also.

"I have never heard of that custom before," said Sancho, "and I'm not going by it. Besides, I have no sword and I've never had one in my life."

"We can get over that difficulty," said the other. "We have a couple of linen sacks, and if we put half a dozen good-sized stones in them, I bet we can pound each other quite handsomely."

But Sancho still objected, saying it was unchristian for two friends who had just been eating and drinking together to begin knocking each other about when they had no reason to quarrel.

"Well, if that's all," said the other squire, "before we get started I'll just come up and knock you down with a few blows and that will make you feel mad enough."

"If you try that, I know how to stop you with my cudgel," answered Sancho. "I am a man of peace, but a cornered

THE SQUIRE HAD A MONSTROUS SNOUT,
COVERED WITH WARTS AND BOILS.

cat can fight like a lion. God only knows what a cornered man like me might do."

"Well," said the other, "let's wait for daylight and see what is going to happen."

When day broke at last and there was enough light to see by, Sancho beheld to his terror and amazement that his brother squire had, instead of an ordinary nose, a monstrous snout that looked like the hooked beak of a bird of prey, covered with warts and purple boils, hanging down past his mouth. Sancho, who was trembling from head to foot, made up his mind that he would endure anything rather than fight such a monster.

Meanwhile Don Quixote took the measure of his adversary and saw he was a sturdy man of middle height, likely to be a strong opponent. His visor was down, so he could not see his face. Over his armor was a tight-fitting gold tunic, decorated with moon-shaped pieces of silvered glass. His helmet had a plume of green, yellow and white feathers. After a brief meeting, the two knights each rode off a short way and prepared to charge the other.

At this moment Sancho ran up and clung to his master's stirrup, begging him not to leave him alone with the nose-monster. Rather than that, he asked Don Quixote to help lift him up into one of the trees where he could observe the com-

THE FORCE OF DON QUIXOTE'S CHARGE

WAS IRRESISTIBLE.

bat in safety. Don Quixote admitted the nose was a fearful sight that probably would inspire terror in anyone other than him, and helped his squire get safely seated among the branches. Then he turned to face his enemy.

Now this stranger was none other than Sampson Carrasco, the scholar of the University of Salamanca, who was masquerading as a knight-errant and who figured on having an easy victory over Don Quixote. He had therefore added to the conditions of the combat that the loser must return home. But Sampson had made a great mistake in selecting his horse, which was an even worse hack than Rocinante. It happened that as the knights rode toward each other, Sampson's horse stubbornly came to a complete standstill, just at the moment when the most speed was needed in order to withstand the force of Don Quixote's charge. That shock was irresistible to Sampson, who flew over his horse's rear and landed heavily on the ground, half stunned.

Don Quixote jumped promptly from his charger and opened the visor of the fallen man to see if he was still alive. What he saw amazed him, for it was the familiar face of his friend Sampson Carrasco!

"Come here, Sancho," he called. "Behold again what wizards are capable of doing."

Sancho came running up. "My advice is that your worship run your sword though his throat, for by doing so you destroy one of your enemies, the enchanters."

"That is so," said Don Quixote. "And the fewer enemies one has the better." He was drawing his sword as the squire of the fallen knight ran up and called out, "Take care, Don Quixote! This man is your friend Sampson Carrasco and I am Thomas Cecial, from your own village, whom you know very well."

"Blessed Virgin!" shouted Sancho. "It truly is Thomas Cecial! But where is your nose?"

"Here it is," he said, as he drew a cardboard mask from his pocket. "And I'll tell you about it, but first we must see to Master Sampson."

By that time, the Knight of the Mirrors had come to his senses and Don Quixote, with his sword point on Sampson's throat, demanded that he admit Dulcinea del Toboso surpassed Casildea de Vandalia in beauty and go to the city of Toboso to put himself at her disposal, or accept death that instant.

The knight answered: "I confess that the dirty shoe of Lady Dulcinea del Toboso is superior to Casildea, and I promise to do all you command me to do."

"You must also swear that the knight you conquered was not myself, but someone resembling me, and I likewise will say that you are not Sampson Carrasco, who you truly do greatly resemble, but someone else."

"I swear everything exactly as you wish me to," said Sampson. "Now let me get up if I can."

They got Sampson on his legs, and his squire helped him to a shady spot where his injuries could be examined and his bruises tended to. Sampson lay there and cursed and moaned and regretted the bad luck that had fallen on his plan to cure Don Quixote of his folly. But now he swore to himself that he would get even with him yet and satisfy his feeling for revenge.

Meanwhile Don Quixote and Sancho resumed their journey toward Saragossa, the knight elated over his victory and the squire in doubt over whether the Knight of the Mirrors and his squire were transformed devils or really and truly Sampson Carrasco and Thomas Cecial, their old friends and neighbors.

"It is strange, your worship," he said, "that those two should look so like men we know, and I cannot help but suspect that they may be the same men."

"How can that possibly be?" replied Don Quixote. "How can it be imagined that my good friend Carrasco would come out armed against me, with the harmless Cecial as his squire, whom I have never insulted in any way? Trust me, Sancho, this is another trick of the wicked magicians who dog me, only this time the trick has failed."

"But why should magicians take the form of those two men instead of any others in the world?" asked Sancho.

"That is easy to explain," answered Don Quixote. "Their devilish minds allowed them to understand that I might be victorious in spite of all their power. So the enchanter cunningly assumed the appearance of my friend so that he might escape with his life if that happened. This trick of transformation is one of their favorites. You remember how successfully they played it off on me when the Lady Dulcinea del Toboso and her handmaidens came to visit me outside Toboso."

That example did not resolve the doubts in Sancho's mind in favor of the magicians because he knew how little magic was at work in that particular transformation. But he had to keep silent about that, and contented himself with the thought that "God knows the truth about everything."

The Adventures of
Don Quixote

PART 2

CHAPTER 10

The Gentleman in Green, Adventure with the Lions, and Astonished Friends

B Y AND BY THEY WERE OVERTAKEN BY A GENTLEMAN mounted on a very fine mare. He wore a long green riding coat, and his whole outfit gave the impression of a country gentleman of taste and importance. His courteous greeting of Don Quixote was courteously returned, but the customs of politeness could not prevent the gentleman from staring in amazement at the strange figure of the knight. Don Quixote saw this and said: "I see your worship is surprised at my appearance, which is unusual in these days. I am a knight of the old school of chivalry, which I am trying to revive. For that purpose I have left my home, mortgaged my estates, abandoned all ease and pleasure, and taken up a life of adventure, enduring all sorts of good and ill fortune in the noble work of helping widows, orphans, damsels in distress, and generally combating injustice. In this task I have earned some reputation, for I learn from a friend of mine, a graduate of Salamanca, that a book has been written about me and thirty thousand copies have been printed. If heaven spares me, many more may be printed in the future. I am, sir, Don Quixote de la Mancha, otherwise known as the Knight of the Sorrowful Countenance. And now that you know who I am, you can stop wondering at my appearance."

The gentleman in green remained silent for some time and finally said: "You are right, sir, in thinking that I was surprised at your appearance, but I confess that what you say about yourself causes me still greater surprise. I had no idea there were now, or ever were, cavaliers riding about righting wrongs and enforcing justice. Or that histories of their deeds are published. I am astonished that it is so. I can only thank heaven that a genuine history such as yours will expose the lying, mischievous fables that have been printed about imaginary knight-errants and their ridiculous, impossible exploits."

"There is a lot to be said on the matter of the truth of those histories," answered Don Quixote.

"Is it possible that any living soul does not know they are false?" interrupted the gentleman.

"Sir," replied Don Quixote, "if we travel together, I hope in time to convince you that you yourself are deluded."

The gentleman, looking hard at Don Quixote, began to suspect that he was not in his right mind. Before they went further, Don Quixote asked to know more about the person he was talking to. The traveler said he was a gentleman of good family and a fair-sized estate, that he had a love of sports and a taste for literature and conversation, and ended up by inviting Don Quixote to dine with him at his house, which was in the village they were headed towards. Don Quixote agreed and they rode on, talking about moral, social and literary topics. The gentleman became more and more astonished that a man of Don Quixote's intelligence should believe in knight-errantry, magic and enchanters.

Suddenly the knight cried out, "Sancho! Give me my helmet. If I am not mistaken, something is about to happen that will require me to interfere with my weapons."

The gentleman looked all around but could see nothing but a cart carrying some large crates, drawn by a team of mules and flying three royal flags to show that it was the property of the king.

Don Quixote planted himself in the middle of the road and yelled to the two men on the cart. "Where are you going, friends, and what have you on the wagon?"

"The wagon and mules are mine," said one of the men, "but the crates contain two fierce lions, presents to the king from the governor of Oran in Africa. They are the biggest lions that ever came to Spain."

"I am not scared of lions," declared Don Quixote, "however fierce or big they are. Open the cages and let them out, and I will show the enchanters who have sent them what Don Quixote de la Mancha can do."

The men on the cart were dumbfounded at this command. Sancho wrung his hands in despair. The gentleman in green urged Don Quixote not to continue with his purpose.

"These lions are not sent to harm you or test your courage," he said. "They are presents to His Majesty and you have no right to interfere with them."

"Let everybody mind his own business!" said Don Quixote. "Mine is to deal with these lions. Now, sir, open the cages at once or I will fasten you to your wagon with my lance."

The terrified man, seeing that Don Quixote was determined, and probably crazy, said, "For God's sake, sir, let me unhitch my mules, for if they are killed by the lions I am ruined."

This Don Quixote allowed. The wagon driver, calling on all there to bear witness that he was being forced against his will and over his protests, unyoked his animals and led them out of harm's way. The gentleman in green, after trying again uselessly to reason with Don Quixote, also went off some distance, taking the tearful, trembling Sancho with him. The man left on the wagon also made an appeal, but got only a stern command to open a lion's cage as an answer. While he set about this, Don Quixote dismounted and turned Rocinante loose, having resolved to fight the lions on foot with his sword. Then he commended himself to God and to Dulcinea, and stood ready in front of the lion's door.

The keeper, seeing no other way, opened the door of the cage and revealed a magnificent lion stretched out on the floor of the crate. Dazed by the sudden flood of light into his den, the lion turned around, reached out an enormous paw and stretched his body its full length. Next he opened his mouth and yawned leisurely. After this he got up and quietly surveyed the landscape. He extended his scarlet tongue, which was two-hands long, and began to lick the dust from his eyes and face. Then he stuck his head out the doorway and gazed calmly around, his great eyes searching, terrifying to even the bravest heart.

Don Quixote, undaunted, waited with impatience for the lion to leap out so that he might engage him and slice him to pieces. But that moment never came. The majestic lion, seeming satisfied with what he had seen, turned back into his den without noticing the knight, slowly lay down again, and went back to sleep.

Don Quixote ordered the keeper to excite the lion by poking him with sticks and beating him, but the keeper refused, saying that the knight had already proven his courage and that he should not force combat on an unwilling opponent.

The knight admitted the truth of this argument. "Shut the door then, and I will signal my friends to return," he said, tying a white cloth to the tip of his lance and then waving it for Sancho and the gentleman in green to see.

"I'll be hanged if my master has not defeated the king of the beasts!" exclaimed Sancho, and he ran forward to learn what had happened.

The keeper gave a full and flattering account of what had taken place. Don Quixote gave him a couple of gold coins for him and his companion as a reward for their trouble. "And if the matter should come to the ears of the king," he added, "and he should wish to know who performed this feat, tell him it was Don Quixote de la Mancha, now known as the Knight of the Lions, for I am dropping the name 'Sorrowful Countenance,' and adopting the other as the customs of chivalry allow."

The gentleman in green, who was named Don Diego de Miranda, had remained silent all this time. Don Quixote turned to him now and said, "No doubt, sir, you consider me extravagant and mad, but I am not as crazy as my actions seem to indicate. Remember there are various sorts of knights–knights of the tournament, knights of the court, knights of the battlefield. Superior to all of these is the knight-errant, who endures hardship to help the poor and the friendless, fearless of wild beasts, ghosts, dragons and magicians. I am a knight of that order and must not shrink from any danger which comes to me in the course of my duty. That was obviously the case with the lions, though of course that action showed an excess of audacity. But it is better to err on the side of rashness than to sink into cowardice."

"There is a good deal in what you say," answered Don Diego, "but we have lost time. Let us quicken our pace and you can rest soon at my house." Don Quixote courteously agreed and they reached Don Diego's mansion at about two in the afternoon.

Don Diego's wife and son came out to meet the party and seemed astonished to see the knight-errant. "Madame," said Don Diego, "this is Don Quixote de la Mancha, the wisest and most valiant knight-errant in the world." The lady, whose name was Dona Christiana, welcomed him kindly and Don Quixote in return kissed her hand gracefully. A similar ceremony was made with the son, Lorenzo, and then the knight and his squire retired to their rooms to prepare for a banquet.

While the knight was washing, Don Diego explained to his wife and son how he had met Don Quixote and described his extraordinary conduct. "I can only say," he concluded, "that while he can talk like a man of sense, he is capable of acting like a madman of the most outrageous kind."

For four days Don Quixote and Sancho enjoyed themselves at the hospitable mansion of Don Diego. Then the knight asked permission to depart, for rest is allowable to knight-errants, but idleness and ease are not. Before going on to Saragossa to the fair, Don Quixote wished to explore the mysterious cave of Montesinos and discover the source of the

HE WAS FINALLY RAISED UP AGAIN TO THE SURFACE.

lakes of Ruydera, both of these places being in the vicinity. After a ceremony of leave-taking, he and Sancho, their packs now resupplied, went on their way well satisfied with their visit.

Their next adventures were not very exciting. They visited the cave of Montesino, where Don Quixote had himself lowered to a great depth. There he fell asleep on a ledge of rock and dreamed of an enchanted world where he recognized Dulcinea exactly as she had appeared when Sancho pretended he saw her near Toboso. When he was finally raised up again to the surface, he insisted it was all real and had never been just a dream at all.

And once at an inn they were being entertained by a puppet-show when Don Quixote entirely lost his reason and slashed to bits some cardboard figures of Moors who, as the story went, were carrying off a lady despite her resistance. For this he had to pay the puppetmaster (who was none other than Gines de Pasamonte in disguise) quite handsomely.

As they made their way on to Saragossa, at last free from such embarrassments, they came to the banks of the river Ebro, where they found a small boat tied by a rope to a tree, but without oars or a rudder. Don Quixote looked up and down the river but saw no one to whom the boat might belong.

HE SLASHED TO BITS SOME CARDBOARD PUPPETS.

"Sancho, this boat, without a doubt, has been sent here in order for me to be carried some distance to aid some imprisoned or bewitched knight, or some other important person. This practice is clearly described in the books of chivalry, though sometimes the enchanter uses a cloud or a dragon to transport the knight who will perform the rescue. Since this is the case, tie the beasts here on shore, for we must trust heaven and use this enchanted boat. All the prayers of all the barefooted friars in the world cannot prevent me."

"In that case," Sancho said, "I see no point in trying to persuade you against it. My duty as a servant is merely to obey your orders. But for the sake of my conscience, I must say that I believe this boat has nothing to do with enchanters and probably belongs to a fisherman."

Together they got in the boat, untied the rope, and drifted downstream. When they had gone a few yards, Don Quixote said that their rate of speed was near a thousand miles an hour and they might soon cross the equator. But Sancho did not agree because he could still see Rocinante and Dapple tied to a tree, and hear them, too, complaining in their own language against being left behind by their masters.

Soon the boat drifted within sight of some flour mills built in the river. Don Quixote turned to Sancho, saying, "See! There is the fortress where the unfortunate knight is held cap-

ROCINANTE AND DAPPLE COMPLAINED IN THEIR OWN
LANGUAGE AGAINST BEING LEFT BEHIND.

tive–or it may be a queen or princess–to whose rescue I am being carried by this boat."

"The only thing I see are water mills where they grind wheat into flour," answered Sancho.

"I believe you think so," said Don Quixote. "No doubt they appear to you to be water mills, but they are not really so. By now you should understand the powers enchanters have to alter things, not to change their substance, but to change their natural appearance into something else. You remember how they changed Dulcinea."

Sancho made no reply, partly because he would have remained silent in any case to this reminder, and partly because he saw that they were gaining speed and headed directly into the dangerous machinery of the mills. The millers, seeing the chance of catastrophe, rushed out of the building all covered in white flour from their work and began using long poles to push the boat away, yelling abuse at Sancho and Don Quixote as they staved them off.

"Just as I told you, Sancho," said Don Quixote, "see the white demons that have come out to oppose us. They do not scare me." Saying this, he stood up in the boat and began waving his sword. "Villains! Release your captive, for I, Don Quixote de la Mancha, the Knight of the Lions, have come to the rescue!"

Sancho fell on his knees in the boat and began to pray. The mill workers struggled to keep the two strangers from being drawn under the great revolving water wheels, and they succeeded, but only by upsetting the boat and spilling its occupants into the water. They were rescued from drowning with difficulty, while the boat was carried into the wheels and smashed to bits.

The owners of the boat now appeared and, demanding to be paid for it, began stripping Sancho's clothes off in order to get some guarantee of satisfaction. The knight, dripping wet, thought it wise now to talk to the enemy. Coolly and self-confidently, he said he would pay for the boat if the prisoner in the castle was delivered to him without a ransom or delay.

"Crazy man!" exclaimed one of the mill workers. "What prisoner and what castle are you talking about? Do you want us to give you our customers?"

This question threw Don Quixote into deep thought. "This crowd," he announced, "is composed of the dregs of humanity, those incapable of generosity. Moreover, it is clear that wicked sorcerers are at work here, frustrating my kind intentions. One enchanter gives me a boat, another destroys it and endangers my life. Heaven help me! There is nothing but plots and more plots. I can do no more here."

THE MILL WORKERS STRUGGLED
TO KEEP THE TWO STRANGERS FROM DROWNING.

Then, turning toward the mill, he said, "Friend in the castle, whoever you are, pardon me for not being able to free you. It is my misfortune as well. But fate has decreed that some more worthy knight shall have that noble task."

Sancho paid for the boat out of what money they had, noting that a few more such adventures would leave them with no money at all. Then he and his melancholy master made their way back to where their animals were tied, leaving the mill workers and fishermen standing in perplexity.

CHAPTER 11

The Duke's Hunting Party, a Reception, Sancho and the Duchess

DEPRESSED IN SPIRIT AND IRRITABLE, THEY REACHED
and mounted their beasts and silently rode away
from the river. The knight was lost in thought about
magicians and his hopeless love. The squire was thinking
about their shrinking supply of money, his master's madness,
and the fading prospect of his being made the governor of an
island.

They rode out of the forest at sunset and came upon
a hunting party which included the charming figure of a

young lady, richly dressed and carrying a hawk on her gloved left hand.

"Run to her, Sancho," said Don Quixote, "and present my compliments. Inform her that I, the Knight of the Lions, beg to be allowed to kiss her hands and to serve her to the utmost of my power."

Off went Sancho on this mission. When he reached the lady he threw himself off Dapple and dropped to his knees, saying, "Lovely lady, yonder cavalier, who goes by the name of the Knight of the Lions, formerly called the Knight of the Sorrowful Countenance, is my master. He has sent me, his squire, Sancho Panza, to beg that he may be permitted the happiness to approach your grace and pay his respects."

"Truly, good squire," said the lady, "you have delivered a very courteous message. Rise, for it is not proper that the squire of a knight so great as the Knight of the Sorrowful Countenance, whom I have heard of, should remain kneeling. Tell your master that both I and the Duke, my husband, will be pleased to have the honor of his company at our country house close by."

Sancho arose, admiring the beauty of the lady, as well as her courtesy, and pleased that she had heard of the Knight of the Sorrowful Countenance, even if she had not heard his latest title.

"Tell me, squire," said the lady, "is not your master the one about whom they are just now printing a book called *The Adventures of Don Quixote de la Mancha*, and whose lady is Dulcinea del Toboso?"

"It is the same, and if it please your ladyship, the squire who is mentioned in that history by the name of Sancho Panza is myself, or I have been changed in the cradle–I mean in print."

"I am very pleased," said the Duchess. "Go tell your master he is welcome in our house and that nothing could have happened to give me greater pleasure."

Sancho joyfully returned to his master, repeated all the lady had said, and praised her beauty and courtesy to the skies using his country-style expressions. Don Quixote sat up tall in his saddle and advanced towards the Duchess with a dignified bearing. She, meanwhile, had informed her husband of what had happened and, as they had both read what had been written about the knight, they agreed to humor him and treat him as a knight-errant should be according to the books of chivalry.

As Don Quixote rode up, Sancho hurried ahead so that he could help him dismount by holding down the stirrup on the off side. But, unfortunately, in his haste to get off Dapple he got his foot tangled in a rope attached to his saddle and soon was hanging with his feet upwards and his face on the ground. Don Quixote, unaware of Sancho's catastrophe and assuming he was at his proper post, began to dismount, intending to do so in the most graceful manner possible. But his saddle turned under his weight, and he was promptly thrown to the ground, where he lay venting his sense of shame by muttering curses on his squire. The Duke sent his servants to help the knight, who was now limping from his fall, and expressed his own concern over the accident.

"There can be nothing unfortunate in an occasion which introduces me to your grace and the incomparable lady, your wife," said Don Quixote.

"Softly, good Don Quixote!" exclaimed the Duke. "As long as Dulcinea del Toboso lives, you cannot very well say that any other lady is incomparable."

Here Sancho decided to interject a comment. "When a potter has the knack of throwing good pots, he can turn out quite a number in a row, and I expect it is the same in nature. I can swear her highness is every bit as good-looking as Lady Dulcinea."

"No knight-errant in the world has ever had such a babbling squire as I am plagued with," said Don Quixote. "Please, your ladyship, take no notice of him."

"If he is talkative I shall like him better," she replied, "for he may use original expressions which will interest me."

The party now set out for the Duke's country castle with the Duke himself riding ahead to arrange a suitable reception for such a famous knight. When Don Quixote arrived he was met by a crowd of attentive servants, who called him the Prince of Knights, sprinkled him with perfumes, threw a fine scarlet cape over his shoulders and escorted him into the mansion with music.

In the large hall they entered, hung with tapestries, he was made the object of more ceremonies. Six maidens took off his armor and would have completely undressed him, in order to change him into finer clothes, if his modesty had not opposed them. Finally he was allowed to escape to apartments assigned to him and Sancho, where he put on the splendid clothes the Duke had given him. Then he strapped on his sword and, with his new scarlet cape over his shoulders and a green satin cap on his head, he returned again to the large hall, where dinner was served.

In spite of his protests he was seated at the head of the table. During dinner Don Quixote was coaxed into explaining his theories of knight-errantry, magic, spells, etc., and into telling of his personal exploits, all of which he did with seriousness and modesty. Sancho occasionally added remarks of his own, which the company found very amusing and Don Quixote found very annoying. One comment touched on the

DON QUIXOTE WAS MET BY A CROWD WHO CALLED

HIM THE PRINCE OF KNIGHTS.

promise his master had made to find him the governorship of an island, and how there were no prospects that the promise might be fulfilled, though Sancho believed it one day would be, if he lived long enough.

Hearing this, the Duke declared, "Sancho, you shall not be disappointed, for in the name of Don Quixote, I promise you the governorship, which is now vacant, of one of my islands."

"Kneel, Sancho," ordered Don Quixote, "and kiss his excellency's feet for the great favor he has done you."

Sancho did so gratefully and with haste. But there was a priest, the chaplain of the family, who had been murmuring throughout dinner and who now stood up from the table, saying he could no longer be a part of fooling with a couple of lunatics, and left the room with his dinner unfinished. The Duke and Duchess made light of his exit and Don Quixote commented on the lack of understanding of some narrow-minded people.

When dinner was over, Don Quixote retired to take a nap. The Duchess took Sancho to her rooms for a private conversation. She challenged Sancho to tell his true opinion of his master's sanity and the real facts about what had happened in the Dulcinea episode outside Toboso. He frankly admitted that his master—who he said was one of the noblest

THE DUCHESS TOOK SANCHO TO HER ROOMS

FOR A PRIVATE CONVERSATION.

men in the world–was indeed crazy where some matters were concerned, but wise on some others. As to the Toboso affair, he confessed that he had tricked his master and he told her ladyship all the details of the business.

"From what you say, Sancho," remarked the Duchess, "you must be as crazy as your master to believe his promises of promotion. It makes me think it would be unwise to give you the governorship of an island."

"I am as mad as my master in many ways," answered Sancho, "and if I have been a fool to believe my master about the island, I have been a greater fool to follow him around the country on this knight-errant nonsense. But I know he means honestly by me and I love him well. I will stick with him through thick and thin, whatever happens. As for the island, I am sure he meant it sincerely, though I've never felt certain about getting it. Even now, if I don't get it because I am a fool, I have enough wisdom not to care about it. I have lived without it since I was born and when I die it will be easier for Sancho the squire to get into heaven than Sancho the governor."

"You certainly shall have the island," said the Duchess, "because the Duke will not go back on his word, and as for the rest of it, you will make a good governor if you do what you think is right and just."

"As for that," replied Sancho, "I am naturally good-natured and fair-minded, but I cannot put up with rogues. The best thing is to make a good beginning, and if I succeed at that I shall be as good a governor as I am a squire."

"Quite right. But to return to the matter of Dulcinea, I have reason to suspect that you were a mere tool in the hands of the magicians and as deceived by their illusions as was your master. It appears likely that the country girl who vaulted so nimbly onto the back of her mule was no other than Lady Dulcinea herself. She may yet turn up in her true shape and convince you that you were even more deceived than your master on that occasion."

"Lord bless us!" shouted Sancho. "I never thought of that! Now I begin to see that my master spoke truly when he said he saw Lady Dulcinea in the cave of Montesinos exactly as I pretended she appeared to me on the road outside Toboso. Come to think of it, how could my stupid head have thought up, on the spur of the moment, so many details of her appearance unless the magicians had been at work on me? And how could my master be so silly as to take my word over the evidence of his own eyes, unless he was also under their spell? But will your ladyship think ill of me for my share in the business? How can a simple fellow like me be on guard against the cunning of those evil enchanters? I thought I was inventing a way to avoid my master's scolding, but all the while I was doing the wicked work of sorcerers! O, God is the judge of everything."

The Duchess reassured Sancho that she did not blame him, under the circumstances. Then she got him to tell what happened at the cave of Montesinos, which was a new story to her. Afterward she sent him away to take a nap. She went to tell the Duke what she had learned and arrange more entertainment for the knight and squire.

CHAPTER 12

The Boar-Hunt,
a Display of Magic,
the Question
of Flogging, and
Good Advice

I T WAS DECIDED TO ORGANIZE A SORT OF THEATRICAL performance on the adventure of Don Quixote at the cave of Montesinos. Five or six days were spent getting ready, and finally a large party set out for the mountains. Events were to start with a **boar-hunt**, and the sport was begun with a tremendous amount of shouting and blowing of horns. Before long a huge boar was flushed from his cover and

BOAR-HUNT
Wild boars are male pigs about three feet tall and five feet long with large menacing tusks. Fierce and dangerous in the wild, they were a favorite animal to hunt for sport.

chased by dogs and hunters in the direction where the Duke and Duchess and Don Quixote were waiting. As the great boar came near, the Duke attacked it with a long spear. Don Quixote raised his shield and drew his sword. Sancho ran and climbed a tree. Unfortunately, he slipped as he was going up and would have fallen, had not his clothing caught on a jagged stump of a lower branch. There he hung suspended and unable to get down without help. But his clothes were gradually stretching from the strain on them, and he roared for help as he continued to droop toward the boar's reach, should it run near him.

But it never did. While Sancho struggled and yelled, hunters speared the boar and killed him. Its carcass was carried on a mule to where a large tent had been pitched for a banquet. The whole party passed the day in gaiety and conversation.

Soon after sunset, the surrounding woods were suddenly lit up as if by magic and trumpets blared, alarming all who were not in on the secret. Then a mounted figure in the costume of a demon came out of the trees toward the Duke's party blowing an enormous horn. Other ghostly figures could be seen moving through the forest.

SANCHO CONTINUED TO DROOP
TOWARD THE BOAR'S REACH

"Ho!" called out the Duke. "Who are you and what
is your business here?"

"I am the Devil," replied the figure, "and I am seeking Don Quixote de la Mancha. Those shadows in the trees
are six companies of magicians, escorting Dulcinea del
Toboso, who, under the protection of the brave French knight
Montesino, comes to inform her knight how she may be freed
from her enchantment."

THE FIGURE PROCLAIMED ITSELF TO BE
MERLIN THE MAGICIAN.

Don Quixote stepped calmly forward. "If you are the Devil," he said, "you should know that Don Quixote de la Mancha stands before you."

"By heaven," exclaimed the demon, "I did not recognize you. Knight of the Lions, I am commanded by the valiant Montesinos to tell you to wait here until he arrives with Lady Dulcinea. May devils have you in their keeping."

"I shall wait and hold this ground, even if all hell attacks me," said Don Quixote to the Duke.

Presently a large wagon rumbled into view, pulled by four oxen with black blankets over their backs and flaming torches attached to their horns. It was driven by two extremely ugly figures, also in black, and carried an old man with a white beard, also dressed in black. He stood up and said, "I am the wise man Lirgandeo," and then sat back down. Next came a similar wagon whose occupant said aloud, "I am the wise man Alguife, the friend of Urganda the Unknown." In a third wagon, a repulsive figure proclaimed itself "Arcalaus the enchanter, mortal enemy of Amadis of Gaul and all his kind." Then came a stately carriage drawn by six pale mules, each ridden by a figure in white holding a burning torch. On a throne in the carriage sat a woman of great beauty dressed in colorful, glittering garments. At her feet sat a male figure in a long robe with a black veil. As they neared and stopped, the figure stood up, threw open his robe and cast off his veil, revealing a horrible image of death, as some people have tried to depict it.

The figure proclaimed itself to be Merlin the Magician, and recited verses to tell Don Quixote how to break the spell on Lady Dulcinea. The solution was to whip Sancho's bare flesh with three thousand three hundred lashes, struck with force.

"NO," SAID MERLIN.

"YOU MUST DECIDE ON THE SPOT."

"What?" yelled Sancho. "Am I to be flogged in order that Lady Dulcinea is not enchanted? The Devil can fly away with that. What has my flesh got to do with her ladyship? If there is no other way of freeing her, then she will die under a spell as far as I am concerned!"

"You ungrateful, garlic-stinking wretch," thundered Don Quixote. "Will you not consent to be flogged for this purpose? Why, I'll tie you to a tree as naked as the hour you were born and give you six thousand six hundred lashes! Say not a word, scoundrel, or I will tear your very soul out of you!"

"The lashes must be accepted freely," interrupted Merlin, "or the method will not work. There is no time fixed for its completion and he may give half the lashes to himself with his own hand."

"I won't have any lashes," shouted Sancho, "whether from my own hand or anybody else's. Why should I be whipped for Lady Dulcinea's sake? It is different for my master; he calls her his life and soul. If anybody's flesh has to be stung for her it should be his. It won't be mine and that is final."

Now the glittering woman in the carriage stood and removed her veil, revealing a face of exceptional beauty. She addressed Sancho:

"Soulless wretch! Crop-eared rascal! Thief! If you were asked to throw yourself from a tower, eat toads and lizards, or kill your wife and children, your squeamishness might be understandable. But to hesitate over three thousand three hundred lashes on your fat carcass, with its gross, filthy hide, is simply amazing. All who hear of this in the future will find it incredible. Look at me with your big goggly eyes, see my tear-washed face and think of the terrible fate from which you alone can save me. Now I can appear as my natural self, but because of your objections I shall be transformed again and my beauty concealed beneath the skin of a coarse peasant girl. Be whipped on that thick flesh of yours and you will be raised from your laziness and gluttony, as well as restore me to my beauty. If that is not reason enough, look on the unhappiness of your master and have compassion on him."

"What do you say now, Sancho?" asked the Duchess.

"I say what I have said before. I will not be lashed. And I should like to ask the Lady Dulcinea where she learned her manner of asking for a favor. She wants me to have my flesh sliced open to please her, and at the same time she calls me names the Devil himself hardly deserves. Does she think my skin is made of brass? Or that I care two straws if she remains under a spell or not? Where are the sweet words and presents she should offer to persuade me? She only abuses me. And my master is just as bad. He threatens me with a double dose of lashes and more names. And besides, they are talking about flogging a governor, not a mere squire. And they come to me just at the time my heart is about to break over the tear in my new clothes caused by that cursed branch. I'd rather turn pagan."

"Friend Sancho," said the Duke, "turn pagan or whatever you please, but you shall not be a governor of mine unless you soften your stubborn heart in this matter. I cannot send my islanders a governor so stony-hearted that he is not moved by beauty, especially over such a trifling matter as these lashes. Really, Sancho, I have to say, no flogging, no governorship."

Sancho, perplexed, waited a while and asked, "Can I have a couple of days to think it over?"

"No," said Merlin. "You must decide on the spot. Lady Dulcinea can leave this place only as her proper self or in the disgusting shape she hates.

"Come, Sancho, be brave," said the Duchess. "Show your gratitude to your master."

"Well, I suppose everyone must be right," said Sancho. "But the Devil take me if I can see why. As for those lashes, I consent on three conditions: I give them to myself whenever I please; I shall not have to draw blood—if some strokes are mere fly-swats, they count all the same; and if I make a mistake counting the lashes, Merlin here must set me right or let the error pass."

"There can be no error of too many," said Merlin, "because the moment the number is reached, Dulcinea will be transformed and will appear to Sancho to reward him. As for mistakes the other way, if they are made honestly and in good faith, they will be forgiven."

"In the name of God," said Sancho, "I will go through with it, but only on the conditions I mentioned."

Instantly, musical instruments began to play, guns went off, and shouts filled the air. Don Quixote embraced his squire. The Duke and Duchess expressed their satisfaction, and Dulcinea curtsied low to her friend Sancho and drove away.

The Duke's steward, who had a flair for such things, had organized and directed the whole performance and played the part of Merlin himself. The next day he had another entertainment ready in which the knight and his squire were tricked into thinking that they had broken a spell of the wicked magician Malambruno, who it seemed had made long beards grow on the faces of several old governesses in the Duke's household.

During the day the Duchess asked Sancho how he was progressing with the flogging necessary to release Lady Dulcinea.

"Madame," answered Sancho, "I have already done five of the three thousand three hundred."

The Duchess asked how he had done them.

"With the palm of my hand, your ladyship."

"But that seems more like slapping than lashing," she said. "You must use a thorny bramble or a knotted whip to satisfy Merlin, otherwise the blows will not count."

"Well, if your ladyship gives me a suitable whip that doesn't hurt too much, I will use it, but I am no rough peasant. My skin is as soft as cotton and there is no reason I should flay myself for the sake of other people."

The Duchess promised to find him a whip and their conversation was ending just as the Duke walked up and asked Sancho what clothes he would need to be a governor, since he was anxious to have him assume the office as soon as possible.

"Your dress must be in keeping with your rank," said the Duke. "It would be unbecoming of a lawyer to dress like a soldier, or of a soldier to dress like a priest. We shall dress you like a scholar and a warrior, for a governor unites learning with arms."

"Clothe me how you will," answered Sancho, "for however it is, I shall always be the same Sancho Panza. As for scholarship, I barely know my ABCs, but I do know how to bless myself. As for arms, I shall try to handle what you give me and make the best use of them I can."

"Well, with such principles and honest intentions you can't go very far wrong," replied the Duke.

At this point Don Quixote joined the group and, hearing that Sancho was to take his new office immediately, asked the Duke and Duchess if he could take Sancho aside in order to give him some private advice. With their permission, he took Sancho back to his own room and sat down beside him to give him a long lecture on the duties and responsibilities of a governor.

"First," he said, "fear of God is the beginning of wisdom and the wise are in little danger of error. Next you must try to know yourself; for every man this is the hardest of all things to do. Remember the story of the frog that wanted to be an ox and do not try to puff yourself up. Remember that you began as a swine herder."

"So I was, but as I grew up I herded geese," said Sancho. "But what does that matter? Not every governor needs to be born as a prince."

"That is so," said his master, who was writing all his words down on paper for Sancho to have later, even though he could not read. "And this is all the more reason for men of humble origins to bear themselves with modesty, so they are not called upstarts and insolent. You need not be ashamed of your ancestors, and if you are not ashamed, no one will try to insult you over it. Do what is right and just and you will have no occasion to regret that you are not a lord. Virtue is a broad sea open to all the world and of greater value than being born to the nobility. Keep your own will in check. Be compassionate to the poor. Be merciful when you can do so without being unjust. Do not let your personal likes and dislikes influence your judgments. Do not be swayed by the tears or smiles of beauty. Do not abuse any man you must punish; it is enough that you must cause him suffering. Remember that we are all sinners and show some consideration even for the most unworthy.

"So much for your moral behavior, Sancho," continued Don Quixote. "Now about your personal habits. First, stay clean and keep your fingernails trimmed. They are not a hawk's talons. Be neat about your dress; carelessness about your clothes will suggest a carelessness in your thought. Avoid eating garlic and onions. Walk with dignity. Speak with deliberation. Eat and drink moderately. Do not chew on both sides of your mouth at once. Don't belch in front of people. That is the best advice in my power to give. God bless your government. I fear your ignorance will cause you to turn your island upside down. Indeed, I wonder if it would not be for the best if I told the Duke frankly that I think you are not fit for the job."

"If you really think that I am not good enough," replied Sancho, "I will give it up at once. I care more for my soul than for my body. And Sancho the simple can live as well on bread and onions as Sancho the governor can on roast chicken, and sleep as soundly, too. Who gave me these ideas except you yourself? I had no more thought of governing an island than does a **bustard.** And if being governor means going to the Devil, I would rather go to heaven as Sancho than hell as governor."

"By heaven, Sancho," replied Don Quixote, "I think you deserve to be the governor of a thousand islands, for, with all your faults, you have character. Without that, knowledge is worthless. Keep to your purpose to do what is right and just in all circumstances."

BUSTARD
A heavy-bodied bird that can fly but most often runs along the ground. Still to be found in Asia, Africa and Australia, it was hunted for food and has almost disappeared from Europe.

CHAPTER 13

Sancho's Island, His Reception and Judgments

THAT EVENING, AS PART OF THEIR PLAN FOR AMUSING themselves with the knight and his squire, the Duke and Duchess sent Sancho with a number of servants to a place that he was told was the island of Barrataria. However, it was in fact a walled village of about a thousand inhabitants that was on one of the Duke's largest estates.

When Sancho's party arrived at the gates of the town, bells pealed out merrily and the people came in crowds to welcome their new governor. First they took him to their church to give thanks to God for his arrival, and, after some ridiculous ceremonies, he was formally given the keys to the town and the title of Perpetual Governor of the Island of Barrataria.

The fatness, the shortness, and the dress of the new governor astonished all those who were not in on the secret about the game being played, and there were many of those.

Finally they took him to the courthouse, seated him in the judge's chair and the Duke's steward addressed him so: "My Lord the Governor, it is the ancient custom of this island for the new governor to answer intricate questions put to him, so that by his answers the people may judge his understanding, and so be either joyful or dejected."

As the steward spoke, Sancho was looking at the wall where a number of large letters were painted, and, since he couldn't read, he now asked what all the writing was about. He was told that it was the record of the date when he became governor, and that it said:

THIS DAY AND THIS MONTH OF SUCH A YEAR, POSSESSION OF THIS ISLAND WAS TAKEN BY LORD DON SANCHO PANZA AND MAY HE LIVE LONG TO ENJOY IT!

"Who is Don Sancho Panza?" he asked.
"None other than yourself," said the steward.

"Please take notice, my friend," answered Sancho, "that I am no don and there never has been a don in my family. I am named simply Sancho Panza, as were my father and my grandfather, and all of us were just Panzas without any dons. Please God, if my government lasts only four days, let it at least get rid of all the dons around here, who must be as annoying as mosquitos. But now for your questions, and I will answer as best I can."

Just then two men entered the court, one looking like a country bumpkin and the other apparently a tailor, since he carried a pair of tailor's scissors in his hand.

The tailor began: "Lord Governor, this good man and I are here because yesterday he came into my shop, put a piece of cloth in my hands, and asked if it was enough to make a hood. I looked at it and said it was. He must have suspected that I meant to steal part of it for myself (basing his opinion on his own dishonesty), for he said he thought there was enough for two hoods. And I agreed there was. Then he went on adding hoods and I kept saying 'yes' until we got to five. Today he called for them and they were ready, but he refused to pay for them. He either wants me to return the cloth or pay him for it."

"Is this correct?" Sancho asked the country man.

"Yes, my lord, but I beg your worship to order him to show the five hoods he made."

TWO MEN PRESSED FORWARD
DEMANDING THAT JUSTICE BE DONE.

"Willingly," said the tailor, as he took his hand out from under his cloak and revealed five little hoods, one on top of each of his fingers and thumb. "On my conscience, I swear I honestly used up all his cloth making them. I am ready to let any expert in the trade examine them."

Everybody laughed at the hoods and the novelty of the case.

Sancho thought gravely for a while and then said, "My judgment is this: the tailor is not to be paid for his work, nor the countryman for his cloth, and the hoods are to be given to prisoners in jail for their benefit. And that ends that case."

Hardly had he finished when two old men, one carrying a walking cane, pressed forward demanding that justice be done.

"My lord," said the first, "some time ago I lent this man ten gold crowns on the condition that he would give them back when I asked. It was a friendly deal, so no writing passed between us and there were no witnesses. Now he says I never loaned him the money, and, second, that if I did, then he has already repaid it. I am sure he never repaid me, but if he will swear on the holy cross before your worship that he did, then I shall forget the matter."

"What have you to say, you with the walking stick?" asked Sancho.

"I admit that I had the money, my lord," said the other, "and, as for the repayment, I agree to the proposal to let the matter be decided by my oath, and I ask to be sworn as he desires."

As the holy cross was being passed to him, he gave his walking cane to his friend to hold. Then, kissing the cross, he solemnly declared that he had returned the money by putting it in his friend's hand. His friend, he supposed, had simply forgotten about the occasion.

Thereupon, the first man, who had always known his friend to be an honest and truthful man, said he himself must be guilty of some strange forgetfulness, and so withdrew his claim for the ten gold crowns. Both men, after bowing politely, left the room.

Sancho had listened attentively to the case and watched the behavior of the men closely. For a long time later he sat with his index finger pressed to his forehead. Then he raised his head and ordered the two men to be brought back. When they returned, he said to the man with the walking stick, "Friend, give me your cane, as I have a purpose for it."

"Certainly," said the old man, handing it to him.

Turning to the man who had loaned the money, Sancho said, "Take this cane and go about your business, for in the name of God, you are now repaid your money."

"Paid, my lord? Surely your worship does not think a cane is worth ten gold crowns?"

"This one is," said Sancho, "or I am a great dunce and unfit to govern this kingdom."

He then ordered the cane broken in two. To everyone's astonishment, out rolled ten gold coins that had been hidden in it. These were handed to the first man and Sancho was admired by all as a second **Solomon**. In response to the compliments showered on him, Sancho explained that he had been struck by the way in which the man with the cane passed it to his friend. That prompted him to remember a story once told by his parish priest about a cane with money hidden in it. When

SOLOMON
King of the ancient Hebrews, the son of David. He was so famous for his wisdom that his name is now almost a synonym for it. One story tells of how King Solomon ordered a baby cut in half to settle a dispute between two women over which was its mother. Solomon believed he could learn which was the real mother with such a command because the real mother would give up her claim rather than see her baby killed.

he got the cane in his own hands, its weight convinced him the gold crowns must be in it and he felt sure of his ground in ordering it broken. Thus the affair ended and one man went away grateful and the other disgraced.

CHAPTER 14

A Feast, Alarming News, and What Makes a Good Diet

WHEN HIS DUTY AS JUDGE WAS DONE FOR THE DAY, Sancho was conducted to the public hall, where a lavish banquet was set up. Music burst forth as he entered and four pages, richly dressed, ran up with basins and towels to wash his hands. When he was cleaned up, he took his seat at the head of the table. There he sat in solitary grandeur, for, although the table was laid out with an abundance of food, no other places were set and no one seemed ready to share in the governor's meal. A doctor was stationed near Sancho's chair, as was someone who appeared to be a chaplain. The chaplain said grace, a servant put a lace napkin around Sancho's neck, and the butler placed a generous helping of food before him.

Sancho was very hungry and was about to make a vigorous attack on the dish when, after a signal from the doctor, it was whisked away by a servant. Before Sancho could recover from his surprise another tempting dish was set in front of him. He had scarcely begun when again the doctor waved his hand and away went the food once more.

Sancho, astonished and annoyed, demanded to know why this was happening and whether he was supposed to be eating dinner or watching a magic show.

"My lord," said the doctor, "it is customary and proper to use the greatest caution about food offered to persons in your exalted position. I, as your physician, have the heavy responsibility of seeing that your lordship eats nothing that may interfere with your digestion or be harmful to your health. The two dishes I ordered taken away were not, in my opinion, good for you. One was cold and watery and the other hot and spicy."

"Very good," said Sancho. "I see a beautiful roast partridge over there which I'm sure will agree very well with me. Pass it up."

THE DOCTOR WAVED HIS HAND
AND AWAY WENT THE FOOD.

As a servant hurried to obey the order, the doctor intervened. "Stop!" he cried, "Not while I have the power to prevent it shall your worship eat that."

"And why not?" asked Sancho.

"As the great **Hippocrates** himself said, 'Omnis saturatio mala, perdicis autem pessima,' which means, 'all eating to excess is bad, but overeating partridge is the worst.'"

"If that is so," said Sancho, "shorten this business by looking at the dishes on the table and pick out what I may eat. Stop waving your wand between the food and my stomach, for I am dying of hunger and to starve a man to death is not a good way to preserve his health."

"Quite right, your excellency," said the doctor. "And I will say you must not eat those stewed rabbits or that veal."

HIPPOCRATES
An ancient Greek physician who is considered to be the father of medicine because he separated it from superstitious beliefs and based it on observation and reason. Doctors often pledge themselves to follow the ethical rules for their profession that are set out in the Hippocratic Oath.

"How about that fine smoking dish of Irish stew?"

"Away with it!" cried the doctor. "Don't think about it for a moment. I cannot permit it. Irish stew! It is the worst thing in the world for someone like you. It's good enough for crowds at a country wedding, but not for governors of islands.

What I can recommend to your worship are those pasty rolls and a few slices of **quince**."

On hearing this, Sancho threw himself back in his chair in disgust and looked hard at the doctor. After a moment of silence he asked him, in as calm a voice as he could manage, to tell him who he was.

> QUINCE
> The dry, sharp-tasting fruit of the quince tree, which is native to Asia and the Mediterranean, that is usually used only for jelly or jam.

"I am Doctor Pedro Recio de Aguero, native of Tirteafuera, and a graduate of the University of Ossuna."

"Then," said Sancho in a rage, "listen to me Sir Doctor Pedro Recio de Aguero, native of Tirteafuera and graduate of the University of Ossuna: if you are not out of my sight in a twinkling I will take a stick and break every bone in your body. Begone! Or I will be the death of you!"

The doctor fled in fright and Sancho turned to the servants. "For the love of God, give me something to eat or take back this precious government. What is the good of a government if a man cannot get enough to eat?"

They were about to comply when a special messenger from the Duke arrived with urgent dispatches. The messenger handed the dispatches to Sancho, who passed them to his secretary and instructed him to read them to himself to see if what they contained was of a confidential or public nature.

He reported that they were confidential, and the hall was cleared so the letters could be read out:

> *Señor Don Sancho Panza, I have learned that enemies of mine and of your island are planning a furious night attack. It will be necessary for you to be alert so as not to be surprised. I know through trustworthy spies that four disguised persons on your island are waiting for a chance to take your life because your talents cause them fear. Keep your eyes open and watch the strangers who approach you. Do not eat anything sent to you as a present. I shall send reinforcements if you need them. I count on you to act as is expected of a man of your understanding.*
>
> Your friend,
>
> THE DUKE

Sancho was astonished and alarmed. Turning to the steward, he said, "The first thing to do is to put Doctor Recio in prison. If any one wants to kill me, it is he, and in the worst of ways, because he wants to starve me."

"Nevertheless," said the steward, "it appears you should not eat any of the food on the table here, for it was a present from nuns and you know the old saying about how the devil lurks behind the Cross."

"That is true," answered Sancho. "Let me have some bread and grapes because I can hold out no longer. Besides, I must keep up my strength for those battles that threaten us. That cannot be done on an empty stomach. And you, secretary, write to the Duke and acknowledge his information. Assure him everything shall be done as he expects and pay our compliments to his lady the Duchess and to Don Quixote. Now bring me something to eat and I shall soon show these spies and murderers what it means to meddle with me and my island."

Sancho was at last allowed to eat a good meal. It consisted of nothing better than boiled cow hocks and onions, but he devoured it with such an appetite that it seemed to be made of the choicest delicacies.

"This is the stuff for me," he exclaimed. "I want none of your dainty foods, for I am not accustomed to them. My stomach is used to beef and bacon, and onions and turnips, and Irish stew made up of all sorts of odds and ends. Let everybody understand that. For I am governor of this island and mean to be obeyed in all things, especially those concerning myself and my Dapple. Then I shall be fit to look after this island, to clean it out of vagabonds, cheats and swindlers, and see that all honest folks have their due and that everyone gets equal justice."

All present applauded these remarks.

Sancho finished his meal and then his officers took him on their rounds through the streets of the town, where he had several small adventures and had to deal with suspicious and disorderly persons, such as gamblers, thieves and cheats. He had many chances to exercise his judgment, and in all such cases he showed good sense and wisdom.

CHAPTER 15

A Perplexing Case, Food and Wisdom, Sancho's Abdication

O NE DAY AS SANCHO SAT ADMINISTERING JUSTICE IN the courthouse, a man came before him with what he said was a strange and perplexing case, one involving a question of life or death.

"My Lord, there is a certain river that passes through the estate of a powerful and privileged nobleman, who at his own expense built a bridge over it for the good of the public. Everyone is allowed to use it without paying a toll, except that they must follow one simple rule, which if they break, they pay the penalty of death. On this bridge the nobleman has established a panel of four judges and a gallows. The duty of the judges is to try persons accused of breaking the law. Now the law is this, in its exact words:

> WHOEVER USES THIS BRIDGE MUST DECLARE TRULY, UNDER OATH, WHERE HE COMES FROM, WHERE HE IS GOING AND WHAT HIS BUSINESS IS. IF IT CAN BE PROVED TO THE JUDGES THAT ANY TRAVELER HAS MADE A FALSE DECLARATION OF ANY OF THESE THINGS, HE WILL BE HANGED ON THE GALLOWS WITHOUT MERCY UNTIL DEAD.

"Now, your excellency," continued the man, "this bridge has been used for years by many, many honest people who never complained about the law or feared it. But now a troublesome fellow has come along, a university student, demanding to be allowed across and saying he will take the oath. When the oath was given to him, he said coolly that he is going to be hanged on the gallows before him and that he has no other business!"

"Now, your excellency, the four judges are in a state of consternation. If they let the traveler pass, they will not be doing their duty, because he will have made a false declaration. But if they hang him, they will be guilty of unjustly hanging

THE ADVENTURES OF DON QUIXOTE   183

a man who made a truthful statement. In this dilemma, they have postponed their decision until they can have the advantage of your opinion–having heard of your wisdom–and they sent me to beg you to advise them."

"Of my wisdom I have doubts," answered Sancho, "but I can promise my frankness and goodwill to help the judges to the best of my ability. Perhaps they might hang the end of the man that took the false oath and let the other end go free."

"That would never do, your excellency, because the man cannot be cut in two. To hang one part would be killing both."

"That is true," said Sancho. "I beg you to go over the case again so that I may more thoroughly understand it."

The man did so, and when he finished the governor sat for some time in deep consideration.

At last he spoke and said, "This matter is, after all, not so difficult as it first appears. It is plain the judges cannot give a right decision either way, and whatever decision they make must be wrong. Therefore the real question is this: Which of the wrong ones do they prefer? Although I can neither read nor write, I have a good memory and I recall just now what my good master Don Quixote told me the night before I was sent, as a punishment for my sins, to govern this island. He told me when justice is doubtful I should always lean to the merciful side, and here his words fit the occasion. The reasons for acquitting and condemning are equally balanced, but it is better to spare a life than to take one, all else being equal. So my advice to your judges is to let the traveler go free."

Everyone expressed admiration for this happy decision, and the steward loudly declared that **Lycurgus** himself could not have given a wiser judgment.

"I do not know him," said Sancho, "and never heard of him before; but if he is that sort of man, I have no doubt he is a good eater–which reminds me that it's past the dinner hour, and I say again, feed me well."

> **LYCURGUS**
> Believed by the ancient Greeks to be the author of the laws of Sparta. History cannot say if he was a real person or mythical.

The steward did not have the heart to play another trick on Sancho and gave him a dinner fit for a lord. For once Sancho ate to his heart's content.

Don Quixote, who meanwhile had had occupations enough at the Duke's mansion–sorceries and enchantments and buffooneries–managed to find the time to write a long, fatherly letter to Sancho, in which he said how pleased he was by the good reports about Sancho that had reached him. Sancho had his secretary write a reply, in which he said:

> *I tell your worship this in order that you may not*
> *be surprised by my not having told you before of*

my administration of the island, where I have
suffered more from hunger than ever I did in our
wanderings through the wilds. The Duke wrote
to us the other day to warn us of a plot to attack
the island and murder me. So far I have only
come across one assassin, my doctor, who tried
hard to starve me to death under the pretence of
saving my life. I have gone through plenty of suffering of this kind, but so far have had no fee or
bribe or present of any sort that would allow me
to send your worship any little token of my affection. I go the rounds at night and by day visit the
market. The other night we came upon a pretty
damsel dressed in her brother's clothes and he in
hers, and arrested both. Their father, we learned,
is a respectable widower. My steward fell in love
with the girl and wants to marry her. And I
think the youth would be a good match for my
daughter. Yesterday I took a basketful of rotten
nuts away from a seller in the market and gave
them to school boys, who I know will pick out the
good ones. The seller I banned from the market
for fifteen days. I am mighty pleased to hear the
Duchess has written to my wife. I hope your wor-

ship is getting along well with her ladyship and
the Duke, for if you fell out, what would become
of me? Heaven protect you from enchanters and
may I come safely through my governorship.

Your humble servant,
SANCHO PANZA, THE GOVERNOR

Sancho's forebodings of a short governorship soon
became real, for the time had come to end the elaborate com-
edy of which he was the victim.

One night the whole island was aroused by a tremendous uproar. All sorts of noises were heard. There were shouts
of soldiers, the clang of weapons, blowing of trumpets, the
blasts of guns, ringing of bells, and the boom and rattle of
drums.

Sancho, who was a heavy sleeper, was awakened
sharply from a deep slumber and jumped out of bed in a terrible fright. He opened the door with trembling hands and
looked out to see what was the matter. He saw twenty or more
men with burning torches and swords rushing down the
gallery shouting, "Arm yourself, Lord Governor! The enemy
has landed in overwhelming numbers and is advancing on us.
Lead us against them or the whole island will be ruined."

"What am I to do?" he exclaimed. "I know nothing of arms or fighting! Send for my master, Don Quixote! He understands such business and will soon rid us of our enemies."

"There is no time for faintheartedness or delay," one of them answered. "You must buckle yourself up in armor and lead us to victory, or to death. Here are your armor and weapons. As our governor you must take the position your duty binds you to take."

"God help me! I do not know what to do," said Sancho. "Do what you please with me."

They set to work putting Sancho in some old armor, strapping him up so tightly that he could hardly move a hand or foot. Then the uproar and confusion began again. Lights were put out, shouts and cries were heard and the sound of weapons banging was heard. Sancho was suddenly knocked to the ground, where he lay like a turtle in its shell, or a ship lying on its side. People passed over his body many times, and he was struck many hard blows. It was all he could do to protect his head by covering it with a shield he had been given. The rest of him was bruised and battered by men pretending to be soldiers in a furious fight.

"Oh," thought Sancho, "that it would please God to let this island be taken or rescued so that I might end my suffering one way or another."

THERE HE LAY LIKE A TURTLE IN ITS SHELL.

His prayer was promptly answered. A big fellow jumped on Sancho's body and shouted, "Victory! Victory! The enemy is driven off by our valiant governor!"

"But where is the governor?" asked another.

"Here I am, under your feet," Sancho said feebly. "Lift me up."

When they had him on his feet he said, dejectedly, "Someone bring me a flask of wine. I am choked with dust and my body is turning to water from such sweating." Meanwhile they also took off his armor and put him to bed, where he fast fainted away from fatigue and terror.

At daybreak he awoke and, without saying a word to anyone, dressed himself quietly. Then he went to the stable where Dapple was, kissed his donkey's head and with tears in his eyes said to his faithful companion: "With you I had good company. Happy were my hours, my days, my years, free from serious care. Since I have parted from you for what I thought was better company, I have had nothing but toil and troubles that have tortured my body and worried the very soul out of me. Let me live again the life I left."

As he said this he went about harnessing Dapple and preparing to leave. After he was mounted in the saddle, which he accomplished with some difficulty, he turned to his steward and some others who had gathered around him and said, "Make way, gentlemen, for I am leaving this island and the governorship. I see clearly that I was not born to be a governor, or to defend islands. I can handle a plow and dig and plant and prune better than I can make laws and rule kingdoms. Heaven be with you all! Tell the Duke that I came into this government without a penny and I leave it without a penny, freely and gladly—not many governors can say that."

There was a show of opposition to his leaving, which did include some real regret on the part of the steward, but Sancho would not be delayed from going. All he would agree to was to accept some food for himself and Dapple for their

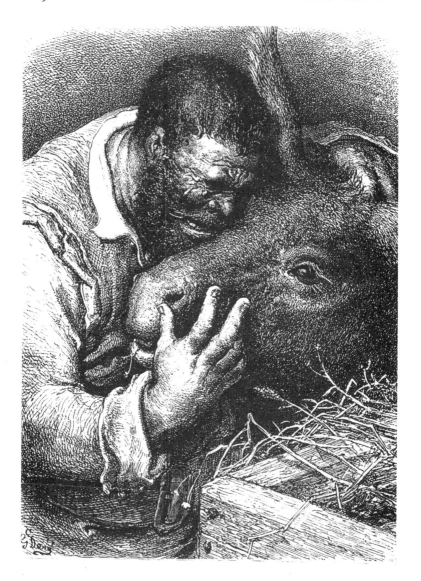

HE KISSED HIS DONKEY'S HEAD WITH TEARS IN HIS EYES.

journey. They wished him a fond farewell, for despite all the nasty tricks they had played on him, they were left with a sincere admiration for his rustic philosophy, his good sense, his faithfulness and his honest heart.

CHAPTER 16

Sancho's Journey, the Pretend Pilgrims, Terror Underground, Departure from the Castle and Stampeding Cattle

SANCHO SET OFF TO FIND DON QUIXOTE, WHOSE company he now thought was better than any governorship.

He had not gone far when he met a dozen sturdy men who looked to be pilgrims and who made signs to him that they wanted charity. He took the bread and cheese he had in his pouch and gave them half of each, but they made more signs demanding money. Sancho gestured to show that he had not a penny and was about to ride away from them when one of the band threw his arms around him and said in plain Spanish, "Why, it is our good friend Sancho Panza, as I am alive and awake."

Sancho looked hard but could not recognize the man.

"What," said the stranger, "don't you know me? Ricote the Morisco–a shopkeeper of your town?"

Sancho looked again and saw now that it was indeed his friend Ricote disguised as a pilgrim. "Why, who could recognize you in this disguise? How is it you are in Spain again after the King's proclamation? It will go hard on you if you are discovered, in spite of the pilgrim's cloak you wear."

"The **Edict** is cruelly hard on us," answered the man. "But I am safe enough with you, and as for others, they are not likely to recognize me in this disguise. When the Edict came out, I made haste to save what I could and seek a new home in another land. First I went to France and then Germany, where I have decided to make my home, near **Augsburg**. I have returned in this

EDICT
A decree by King Charles V in 1525 that expelled all people of Moorish ancestry from Spain.

AUGSBURG
A city founded by the Romans in what is now Bavaria, Augsburg was one of Europe's most important commercial centers in the late Middle Ages.

disguise in order to recover some treasure I buried before flee-ing, and to bring my wife and daughter away with me."

Ricote de Morisco then suggested that Sancho come along to help him, promising to reward him generously. But Sancho declined, being bent on returning to his master. He agreed to accompany his friend to some nearby woods, how-ever, where the pilgrim party had set up a camp, and join in a feast that was being prepared. There was plenty of food and wine, and Sancho enjoyed himself for many hours in excellent company.

It was very late and after a long nap that he finally parted from his friend. He had not got far when he began to feel very sleepy and heavy, due mainly to the good cheer he had drunk with the pilgrims, and also because the night was warm. So he decided to sleep out under the stars, even though he was not far from the castle where he expected to find Don Quixote. But as he left the road to find a resting place among some bushes, Dapple fell into a concealed pit and down went man and beast to the bottom. Fortunately the hole was not very deep and no harm was done, but it was deep enough to prevent the possibility of climbing back out. Sancho only real-ized this after spending a long time groping along the sides in the dark. At last he gave up, hoping to be able to see a way out once there was daylight.

DOWN WENT MAN AND BEAST TO THE BOTTOM.

When morning came at last he found a crevice in the side of the pit that seemed to lead somewhere. With difficulty he crawled through it and found himself in a spacious cavern, dimly lit from cracks in its ceiling. From here other passages branched off. Sancho had no choice but to follow one of these routes, but first, working with his hands alone, he was able to enlarge the crevice enough to allow Dapple to get through.

Long, weary, and fearful was their journey through the dark and winding passages of the cave. The floor was rugged and Sancho's imagination dwelt on the danger of falling again into a deeper level of the cavern and on dreadful ghosts his superstitious mind invented. "Heaven protect me," he said once aloud. "If only this terrible mishap had happened to my master, he would think the whole thing was a grand adventure. He would have filled these dungeons with magicians and knights and damsels. Instead I tremble in every limb because of the darkness and the unknown things that surround me, the chickenhearted soul that I am."

Thus he went on voicing his despair for some time, making what speed he could through the passages. At last he was cheered to see light ahead that seemed to come from some opening into the cavern from the world above. He hurried on and discovered that the opening was too high to be reachable. He shouted and shouted as loudly as he could: "Ho! Ho! Is there any Christian up there who can save a poor sinner from being buried alive?"

He was overjoyed to hear a prompt response, one he hardly expected, and still more astonished and delighted to recognize the voice of his master asking who he was and what was the matter.

The fact was that Sancho, in his underground wanderings, had all the while been progressing toward the castle where Don Quixote had been staying so long. The knight happened to be taking his morning exercise when Sancho's shouts attracted his attention.

It was with considerable consternation that he heard the name and recognized the voice of the underground prisoner as that of his squire. He thought Sancho must have died and be calling him from **Purgatory.**

> **PURGATORY**
> In Roman Catholic teaching, the state that souls destined for heaven first enter after death so that they may be purified of their sins.

"If," said Don Quixote, "you really are my late squire Sancho Panza and—by God's special mercy—you are not in Hell, but in Purgatory, and wish for prayers for your release, I will spare nothing to help you."

"I am your squire Sancho Panza sure enough," Sancho replied. "And I am not dead, but alive. Last night Dapple and I—I quit the governorship of Baratarria for reasons I'll explain later—fell into a pit and we have been wandering around in underground passages since then." Just then Dapple brayed so loudly and clearly that the ground trembled.

"That's enough!" yelled Don Quixote. "I see you are not in Purgatory, but a living Sancho and living donkey. Be patient while I run back to the castle to fetch help."

Don Quixote lost no time telling the Duke and Duchess about Sancho's predicament and a rescue party was sent out. The pit was well-known on the estate and in a very short time, with the help of ropes and pulleys, Sancho and Dapple were pulled out and taken to the castle.

Later in the day Sancho had an audience with his hosts and told them how he fell into the pit and explained why he abandoned his government. "Your graces made me governor of Baratarria not because I deserved it," he said, "but because it pleased you to do so. Naked I entered upon it and naked I came out. I ruled the best I could. I heard cases and gave decisions, all the while suffering from hunger and thirst. We were attacked at night and put in great danger, but we beat our enemies off–or at least that is what I was told. However, all things considered, I came to the conclusion that government is not my line. So I gave it up and yesterday Dapple and I left Baratarria leaving things no better and no worse than before. So here I am condemning governments of all kinds and content to go back to being my master's squire."

This is a summary of Sancho's long remarks, at the end of which the Duke hugged him, said he was a worthy fellow, and promised to give him a place on his estates that was less perilous than being governor. The Duchess was equally kind.

Don Quixote now thought it was time to end his visit and he took the opportunity to ask his host's permission to leave. His request was granted with polite expressions of regret. Early the next morning he sallied forth completely armed, mounted on his steed Rocinante, with Sancho follow-

HE TOOK THE OPPORTUNITY
TO ASK HIS HOST'S PERMISSION TO LEAVE.

ing on Dapple and well-supplied with food. The Duke and Duchess saw them off from the courtyard. Don Quixote courteously waved his lance and bowed his head and then rode away, looking gallant, into the open country to the cheers of those whom he had so long unwittingly amused.

"Liberty, friend Sancho," he remarked after they had gone a little way, "is a great thing in itself–one of the most precious of all human blessings. Ease, luxury, abundance–they are all very well, but when they are due to the hospitality or kindness of others that one cannot return, there is a sense of burden that comes with them that is not agreeable to sensitive minds. Happier is the man who eats his crust of bread by the side of stream without feeling he owes anything for it to anyone."

"All the same," said Sancho, "give me the well-stocked cupboard and snug bed of a castle. I could be happy enough with them. Even without them, I am happy enough with these well-filled bags of food and this purse with two hundred gold crowns in it that the Duke's steward gave me as a parting gift from his master. The castle was good enough for me and I am afraid we will not find as good a quarters elsewhere. Instead, we will come upon poor roadside inns, bad food and rough treatment."

As the knight and his squire talked on they passed into a forest where they came upon a fashionable party from a nearby town picnicking and enjoying themselves at all sorts of sports and games. They had pitched large tents by the side of a stream and were pretending to be shepherds and shepherdesses. They gave the newcomers a hearty welcome, but as soon as they learned that their visitors were none other than the famous knight of La Mancha and his squire, nothing could restrain their pleasure and friendliness. They invited them to stay for a feast that was about to take place in the largest tent, and neither the knight nor the squire could think of a reason to decline.

Don Quixote, despite his protests, was forced to sit in a place of honor, while Sancho glided down the table to where he was better able to help himself to the food.

The knight proved immensely entertaining to the party during supper, giving his unusual views through lofty lectures on ordinary and not-so-ordinary subjects. At the end of the feast, Don Quixote formally and gracefully thanked his hosts for their favors and the honor they did him. He launched into an eloquent speech on the gratitude due to those who show kindness to strangers.

"For my part," he concluded, "I feel bound to show my gratitude for such friendly entertainment in the only way in my power. Therefore, I have resolved to hold the highway near here for two days against all who travel it and compel them to acknowledge that the lady shepherdesses here around me are the most beautiful damsels in the world, except, of course, for Dulcinea del Toboso."

This idea alarmed the party, but amused them as well. They tried to turn him away from his insane plan and the shepherdesses told him he need not go so far in return of the small kindnesses they had shown him. But it was all for nothing. He was firm in his decision and, mounting Rocinante, lance in hand, he went off to the highway leading to Saragossa and waited in the middle of the road.

After a while a bustling crowd of men came along herding a mob of cattle to a town not far away where there was to be a bullfight in a day or two. As they came near and saw the knight blocking the road, they shouted out, "Out of the way, fool! Do you want to be gored and trampled to death by bulls?"

"Rogues!" answered Don Quixote. "I do not fear your bulls, though they are the fiercest that ever bellowed. Admit at once, you scoundrels, that the ladies of this grove are the most beautiful and graceful of all other ladies, or accept my challenge to battle."

The herdsmen had no time for such nonsensical talk from the strange man in the road and before anything more could be done, the herd of cattle overwhelmed Don Quixote

THE CATTLE TRAMPLED THEM HEEDLESSLY
INTO THE DUST.

"YOU EAT, SANCHO," HE SAID, "AND LET ME DIE."

and Rocinante and Sancho and Dapple and trampled them heedlessly into the dust and passed on their way. But no serious injury was done to any of them, and soon Don Quixote was on his feet running after the herdsmen, roaring as loudly as he could.

"Stop, rascals! Turn and face me, singlehanded as I am!"

But the herdsmen ignored him, or perhaps did not hear him, and continued on. Don Quixote chased them until he was exhausted. Finally he gave up the pursuit and returned to his squire walking slowly and dejectedly. He abandoned his plan to hold the road, and, mounting Rocinante and followed by Sancho, rode sadly away, saying nothing to the party in the woods.

In a little while they came to a clear spring in a shady grove and there they tried to clean themselves of the dirt they had recently acquired. Sancho proposed that they eat something, but the knight was too depressed to eat. "You eat, friend Sancho," he said, "and let me die in my grief. Here I am, famous in history, renowned for courtesy and chivalry, sought after by princes, beloved by fair damsels, yet instead of the trophies my exploits deserve, I am trampled into the dust of the road by the hooves of filthy cattle. Eat? Never! Let cruel starvation bring death."

"It is curious, sir" said Sancho soothingly, "how different people feel or see a thing in totally different ways. To me it appears that the best answer to our mishap is a good meal and a sound nap on the soft, green mattress around us. I am sure, sir, if you would only try this remedy, you would wake up a new man." Finally the knight gave in to Sancho's persuasion and ate a little.

"If, O Sancho," he said, "you would do as I ask, my sorrows would be greatly relieved and I could sleep soundly. What I want is your promise that while I rest you will go into the woods and, with Rocinante's reins, give your naked flesh three or four hundred lashes as an installment, long overdue, of the three thousand you have agreed to endure in order to free Dulcinea from enchantment."

"I wish, like your honor," Sancho replied, "to enjoy a good sleep, and what you suggest does not agree with that purpose. There may be things to be said in favor of flogging—everything has its time and place—but lashing oneself in cold blood, as it were, is not an appealing pastime, especially to someone who has such tender skin as mine. So what I say is, let us both settle down to sleep and afterwards trust Heaven for guidance. Her ladyship will have to have more patience and perhaps someday, when she least expects it, she may see a lattice-work of stripes on my back, for I do mean to make good my promise sooner or later."

Don Quixote was not pleased, but he had to content himself for the time being with this vague promise. He pressed the matter no further and soon both the knight and squire were fully enjoying their naps.

CHAPTER 17

Adventure with Highwaymen, the Defeat of Don Quixote

THEY AWOKE LATE IN THE DAY AND RESUMED THEIR journey, except that Don Quixote decided to go to **Barcelona** instead of Saragossa. For six days they traveled easily without incident. But on the night of the seventh day, as they rested in a grove of trees not far from the road, the idea came into

208

Don Quixote's head that it was high time Sancho should wipe off some of the lashes he had promised to take in order to free Dulcinea from her spell. Thinking it would be useless to appeal to Sancho again on the subject, he decided to take the matter into his own hands and himself give a few hundred lashes to Sancho. So, taking Rocinante's reins to serve as a lash, he went up to his sleeping squire and began to unbutton his clothes. Naturally, this woke Sancho up and he asked Don Quixote what was going on.

"I have come to make up for your shameful neglect by giving your bare flesh at least two thousand out of the three thousand and odd you agreed to suffer for my lady's sake. So take off your clothes at once."

"Not I," said Sancho. "The bargain was that I inflict the strokes on myself as I see fit and I mean to stand by that bargain and make others stand by it, too. I am not inclined to lash myself now and so the matter must wait for the future."

"I've had enough of that," said Don Quixote, "and I have no confidence in your doing anything about it in the future." With that he grabbed Sancho, who in a moment had taken Don Quixote around the chest, kicked his feet out from under him and laid him down gently on his back, where the knight was held so firmly that he could not move.

"Traitor!" cried Don Quixote. "How dare you rebel against your rightful master and use violence?"

"I only defend myself," said Sancho, "and I use no more violence than necessary for the purpose. If your worship will promise to leave me alone and leave the whipping matter to me, I will let you up."

After some more discussion the knight agreed and the squire helped him to his feet. Then Sancho went to look for another tree to sleep under. As he rolled under one nearby he became aware of something dangling over his head. Reaching up his hand, he felt a man's legs, with shoes on, swinging above him. Astonished and afraid, he shifted to another tree, where he found yet another pair of swinging legs. Jumping up in terror he ran to Don Quixote, calling loudly, who came to him and heard his story. Together they felt around in the darkness and found not two pairs of dangling legs, but several pairs.

"No doubt," said Don Quixote in a reassuring tone, "officers of the law have been busy around here hanging highway robbers on trees, as they sometimes do by the dozen. There is nothing supernatural about it and you do not need to fear. It is a sign we are near civilization. Barcelona cannot be far off."

Dawn proved Don Quixote to be right; the dangling legs did indeed belong to the bodies of hanged thieves. But

HE FELT A MAN'S LEGS, WITH SHOES ON,

SWINGING ABOVE HIM.

this fact was hardly certain to the knight and his squire when they were suddenly surrounded by some forty living robbers, who told them not to move until their captain arrived. Resistance was useless. Don Quixote's weapons were some distance away and his gallant steed, free of her saddle and bridle, was off grazing among the trees. So they remained still, awaiting what was to come. Not so the robbers, who set to work emptying the pouches and wallets on Dapple. Fortunately, Sancho had taken the precaution of putting his money in a belt around his waist, but even this might not have saved it from the nimble fingers of the robbers had not their captain arrived and interrupted their searching.

He was a fine, robust man of about thirty-four years, mounted on a good horse, clad in armor and armed to the teeth. He was clearly superior to his followers. He approached Don Quixote, politely introduced himself as Captain Roque (he was a famous brigand in those days) and asked for Don Quixote's name.

"Sir," answered the knight, "I am Don Quixote de la Mancha, the world-famous knight-errant, though I must admit to neglecting my duties as a knight in allowing myself to be surprised unarmed and without my horse. Had it been otherwise, my capture would not have been easy for your men."

Captain Roque had heard of the extraordinary character and adventures of Don Quixote and was very pleased to meet him. He treated him and Sancho in a friendly, hospitable fashion and ordered his men to return all the things they had taken from the pair. They had apparently come into the woods to divide the plunder of other robberies and they went on with that task for some time. They were just barely done when one of their scouts came back with the news that a group of travelers was approaching on the highway.

Instantly there was bustle and excitement. The Captain gave orders promptly, with decision, designed to ensure that none of the travelers would escape capture. He did not join his men, but stayed in the woods to talk to Don Quixote, who was surprised to find that this murderer and robber was well educated, came from a good family and had a naturally gentle manner. Revenge and a sense of injustice had brought him into the life he now led.

Don Quixote was earnestly trying to persuade the Captain to abandon his desperate criminal career, which could have only a disgraceful end, when his men returned with their prisoners. Among them were a couple of pilgrims, two infantry officers on the way to join their regiments, a lady and her daughter traveling under the officers' escort, some servants and a couple of mule drivers. The travelers were ques-

DON QUIXOTE URGED THEM
TO GIVE UP THEIR CRIMINAL CAREERS.

tioned by Roque about who they were, why they were traveling, what money or valuables they might have, and so on. In
the end the prisoners admitted to having valuables worth
some nine hundred crowns. After some debate and pleading
it was finally agreed that they would hand over one hundred
and fifty crowns as a ransom. Roque then gave them a written
pass to protect them from being seized by any other member
of his band that they might meet later on the highway. The
travelers then went on their way again, delighted to have
escaped from such serious danger at so little cost.

For three days and nights Don Quixote stayed with
Captain Roque, sometimes hiding, sometimes waiting in
ambush, always watchful and alert. They were excellent company for each other and the captain was especially pleased by
the originality of what the knight had to say.

In the end, Roque and six of his men escorted Don
Quixote at night along back roads into the outskirts of
Barcelona and there parted from him with thanks for the pleasure of his company. Roque was a gentleman by birth who
had taken up his life in the wild woods because of political
persecution. He was not a common robber. He told Don
Quixote that he had sent word to friends in Barcelona to
ensure that Don Quixote would have a good reception from

ROQUE TOLD THEM HE TOOK UP LIFE IN THE WOODS
BECAUSE OF POLITICAL PERSECUTION.

them. As he bid them farewell, Roque gave Sancho ten crowns, and then he and his men rode off.

Their parting took place near the seashore early in the morning. When day broke the knight and his squire saw, for the first time in their lives, the mighty and boundless sea, with the rising sun tipping the rippling waves with gold, the ships at anchor heaving in swells as their flags and pennants fluttered in the breeze. Boats and barges were passing in all directions and the air was filled with the sound of trumpets and drums. It happened to be the day of a naval and military review. In a few minutes a large body of cavalry in brilliant uniforms emerged from the city. Then there was a roar of cannon and gunfire from the ships and the shore and a mock battle began.

Don Quixote and Sancho watched the spectacle with amazement and delight. As the morning wore on in this way, a party of elegantly mounted gentlemen rode up and saluted them. One, who appeared to be their leader, addressed Don Quixote by name and title, and introduced himself and his party as friends of Captain Roque. He was Don Antonia Moreno, a wealthy nobleman of Barcelona. Don Quixote acknowledged the greeting and accepted Don Antonia's invitation to enter the city as his guest.

The party then formed into a procession, led by a band playing music, and headed towards the city, attracting a boisterous crowd that laughed at the outlandish knight and his squire and teased Rocinante and Dapple.

For the next few days Don Quixote was handsomely entertained by Don Moreno at his mansion and introduced to the sights of the city. But the knight was freely made use of as the butt of jokes by his host, too. Many pranks were played at the expense of the innocent gentleman and his squire.

Don Quixote got into the habit of riding down to the shore every morning, fully armed, to exercise and keep up his knightly training. Though always ready for adventures, he was nonetheless surprised one morning to see coming towards him another knight-errant, who bore a shield with a brilliant full moon painted on it.

When the strange knight came within hearing, he called out, "Renowned Don Quixote de la Mancha, I am the Knight of the White Moon, whose incredible exploits you have no doubt heard of. I have sought you to do battle with you, to test the force of your arm, unless you are ready to admit that my lady, whoever she may be, is beyond comparison with your Dulcinea del Toboso. If you will admit this fact you will spare me the trouble of taking your life. If you prefer to fight and I defeat you without killing you, I shall require that you, on your honor, give up being a knight-errant for one whole year. If you triumph and I am at your mercy, then my horse and arms become yours and the fame of all my victories will pass to you."

Don Quixote was momentarily as shocked by the arrogant tone of the White Moon knight as he was by the reasons for the challenge. But in a moment, realizing the seriousness of the situation, he answered calmly:

"Sir Knight of the White Moon, whose valiant deeds I have never heard of before, I venture to swear that you have never seen the beautiful Dulcinea, for if you had, you would not have made this demand of yours. So, without calling you a liar, but merely saying you are mistaken, I accept your challenge, and at once, so that the matter may be settled immediately. I do not desire to have the fame of your exploits because I do not know what they are and I am content with mine, such as they are. Take your ground and let us see who Heaven favors."

As they talked, Don Moreno and some of his friends rode up and wished to know what was the matter. On hearing Don Quixote's explanation they thought some outsider was interfering with their privilege of fooling the knight.

As they stood in a state of wonder, the rival knights wheeled their steeds and made a battleground between them.

At the instant they came face to face with each other they charged forward. The White Moon Knight was better mounted and his fleet horse was in full gallop when Don Quixote had just begun. As a result, the White Moon Knight (who seemed to avoid pointing his lance at Don Quixote) collided against him with such force that Don Quixote and Rocinante were both forced suddenly to the ground.

The victor jumped down and drew his sword, calling on Don Quixote to admit defeat and acknowledge the inferiority of Dulcinea. To which the vanquished knight answered:

"She is no less beautiful because I am unfortunate and unworthy of being her champion. You can take my life, but you cannot kill the truth."

"I do not want either," answered the White Moon Knight. "All I expect of the great Don Quixote is the accepted condition: one year's absence from knight-errantry."

The bewildered spectators urged Don Quixote to accept these favorable terms, which did no insult to Lady Dulcinea and were no more than what he had bound himself by honor to do.

Don Quixote admitted as much and gave his promise to the White Moon Knight, who then galloped away to the city.

Both Don Quixote and his horse were badly hurt by the encounter and lay stretched out on the ground, unable to

THE KNIGHT WAS LIFTED AND CARRIED INTO TOWN
UNDER SANCHO'S CARE.

get up. Finally a chair was sent for and the knight was lifted into it to be carried into town under the care of Sancho, who was as upset over his master's condition as he was over the prospect of an unprofitable year in retirement.

Meanwhile Don Antonia lost no time pursuing the White Moon Knight to find out who he was and what he meant by this mysterious business. He traced him to his hotel and came upon him in his room as his servant was removing his armor. The knight replied frankly to Don Antonia's questions.

"I am Sampson Carrasco," he said, "a friend of Don Quixote, whose madness has long been a cause of distress to his family and neighbors. His folly has excited pity for him from all who know him to be an honorable and generous gentleman. I pledged myself to rescue him by any possible means from his wandering, dangerous life. Rest at home, in the care of his relatives and friends, is his only chance of being restored to reason and health. I could think of only one method to achieve this goal and today I have succeeded in accomplishing it. This is the second time I have tried. The first time I was the worse off from the encounter. Three months ago, as the Knight of the Mirrors, I tried this trick and failed miserably. I was mounted on an unmanageable beast and Don Quixote unhorsed me in a moment. I was hurt so badly I was laid up several weeks. I managed better this time, but now, sir, I must rely on your honor not to reveal what I have told you, for Don Quixote can be counted on to keep his pledge, so long as he does not discover the deception."

"You can rely on me," said Don Moreno, "though I wish the world was not to lose the amusing performances of the knight and his squire."

CHAPTER 18

Homeward Bound, Settling the Flogging Account, Death of Don Quixote

F OR A WEEK DON QUIXOTE WAS CONFINED TO HIS bed under the care of doctors. All the while he suffered from the blackest melancholy, in spite of all the efforts of his host and friends to cheer him up. On the seventh day he was recovered enough from his bruises that he was able to travel and, thanking his Barcelona friends for their hospitality, he set out sadly for home. Sancho had to trudge along on foot, much to his unhappiness, because his master, having

CONFINED TO HIS BED,
HE SUFFERED THE BLACKEST MELANCHOLY.

pledged not to carry arms for a year, passed them to Sancho,
who now had Dapple so laden down he could not ride her.

They journeyed all day at a slow rate and without any
adventures. That night they camped in a wood and ate a
scanty supper. Sancho went off to sleep at once, but Don
Quixote could not rest. His mind brooded feverishly over his
defeat and the poor showing he had made as Lady Dulcinea's
champion. Finally he decided to wake up Sancho, partly for
the sake of having company and partly to beg him again to
begin taking his lashes to end the enchantment of Dulcinea.

HIS MIND BROODED OVER HIS DEFEAT.

It was with some difficulty that he roused Sancho, who remained drowsy.

"You know, Sancho, it is part of the duty of a good servant to share his master's vigils and his griefs, and the solitude of this place this night suggests we should mingle watchfulness with our slumber. The hour and the spot also invite something else, good Sancho—I mean those lashes you have to endure. I ask you to make use of this favorable chance to reduce the account somewhat. Go off a short distance, and with a willing heart and a vigorous hand give yourself three or four hundred lashes for the sake of Dulcinea. I will not wrestle with you again; you are too strong for me. I make the request as a favor."

"Sir," replied Sancho, "I am not a monk, to get up in the middle of the night and discipline myself with lashes. Leave the flogging alone for the present and let me sleep, or you will make me swear never to accomplish the promise I so unwillingly made."

"Soul of stone! Pitiless squire!" shouted Don Quixote. "Is this the return you make to your master for his favors in the past, to say nothing of those to come? Because of me you were made governor of an island. And through me you may yet become a duke, or some other great person, when my year of retirement is over and is followed by a brighter, more glorious time than ever. *Post tenebras spero lucem.*"

"I don't know what that means," answered Sancho. "I only know that when I am asleep I am not bothered by hopes or fears or glory or misfortune. Blessed be the man who invented sleep, I say, for it is a cloak that covers all a man's thoughts,

POST TENEBRAS SPERO LUCEM "After the darkness I expect the light," a quotation from the Book of Job in the Bible's Old Testament.

banishes his hunger, quenches his thirst, drives away his coldness, the very cold that lowers his fever. It is a universal money that buys everything, a counterweight that balances everything, that makes a clown the same as a king, the fool as good as a philosopher. It has only one fault—it is too much like death."

"Why, you are quite eloquent," said Don Quixote. "I have never heard you talk like that before."

Here their conversation was interrupted by a strange rumbling noise that seemed to come from the woods all around them. Don Quixote picked up his sword and stood on guard. Sancho crept under Dapple and fortified himself by putting the saddle on one side of him and Don Quixote's armor on the other. The true cause of the disturbance was a great herd of pigs that was being driven for sale to a distant fair, and it was the noise they and their drivers made that had alarmed Don Quixote and his timid squire. But before they quite understood that, the herd came rushing over them, overwhelming master and man, horse and donkey. Sancho stood up, furious at having been trampled by the dirty pigs. He wanted to take his master's sword and run some of the pigs through, but the knight would not allow it. Don Quixote advised him to go back to sleep, and meanwhile he calmed himself by singing a song. Sancho was soon lulled to sleep by his master's sad tune.

So the night passed, and it was not until the morning sunbeams shone in the face of the squire that he awoke and began to think about breakfast. He soon discovered that the

THE HERD OF PIGS CAME RUSHING OVER THEM.

hogs had destroyed his supplies as they passed through, eating most of them, spoiling nearly all the rest and leaving very little for the homeward journey.

During the day, Don Quixote tried to come to a definite understanding with his squire over the problem of the lashes. "I do not know if it is permissible to pay you to inflict those lashes on yourself, but I think we might risk it, Sancho, if you would tell me what payment would be enough for you and we could make an arrangement."

Sancho admitted that as poor as he was, with a wife and family to provide for, the proposal was tempting. "The lashes to be suffered are three thousand three hundred and thirty-three," he said. "Now, your worship could hardly expect me to value those strokes at less than a penny a piece. Indeed, I could not consider a lower rate. So the whole amount, if my calculations are right, would come out to two hundred and seventy-five shillings, which amounts to thirteen pounds and fifteen shillings, which is hardly fair for all the torture to my flesh, but it is a large sum for man like me. If you agree to the bargain, I can pay myself out of what I am carrying that belongs to your worship and I will return home well-pleased, even though I have been soundly flogged."

Don Quixote immediately agreed to the charge and expressed his eternal gratitude to Sancho for his self-sacrifice. Moreover, he offered to add to the amount if Sancho would begin as soon as possible. Sancho promised to begin that very night and lose no further time.

When it was dark and after they had finished their supper under some trees at the roadside, Sancho made part of Dapple's halter into a vicious-looking whip and stepped about twenty paces into the woods in order to strip and beat himself.

"Be careful, friend Sancho," said the kindhearted Don Quixote. "Do not use too much violence or give way to fury, for it is not necessary to cut your back to ribbons. Take your time between each stroke and I will count them by their sound so that you do no more than necessary."

"GO ON," SAID DON QUIXOTE,
"AND THE PRICE SHALL BE DOUBLED."

"I mean to lay it on smartly," answered Sancho, "but not so much as to kill myself at the beginning, which would spoil the chance of freeing Dulcinea from her enchantment." Then he stripped to the waist and had not given himself even a dozen lashes when he stopped and yelled out to Don Quixote that he had made a mistake in the bargain and that each stroke would have to be worth two pennies at least.

"Go on, friend Sancho," replied Don Quixote, "and the price shall be doubled so long as you have the courage to finish the task."

"Very well. It will now rain down lashes," said Sancho.

And so it did—and every one could be heard distinctly—but the whip did not fall on Sancho's back. Taking advantage of the darkness, he whipped the bark on the trees around him and let out a great howl or groan each time as if he had truly hit himself. His master began to fear he was overdoing it and, coming towards him, called out to him to stop for the present. "You have already given yourself more than a thousand lashes," said Don Quixote. "And that is enough for one session."

"No, no," replied Sancho, "I am not someone who does things halfway, or shrinks from a little pain when it has to be faced. Go off a little farther, your worship, and leave me to do another thousand lashes so that the whole job can be done in just two floggings."

"Since you are in a good frame of mind about it," said Don Quixote, "keep on in Heaven's name, but stop when you feel you have had enough."

So Sancho went back to flogging trees, and with so much force and energy that the beech trees around him were all stripped of their bark one after another. Finally, after a tremendous blow and a corresponding roar from himself, he brought his performance to an end, just as his master rushed up to stop him from going on any further.

"Well, sir," said Sancho, "as you wish, so let it be, and to tell the truth, I have had about as much as I can bear. I am almost flayed alive. Please put your cloak around me so that I do not catch a deadly cold, which I am told often happens to people who have been whipped."

Don Quixote readily gave up his cloak and Sancho coiled up snugly in it. He slept comfortably though the night while his master had to manage with what warmth he could get from his shirt and vest.

The next day Don Quixote insisted, for Sancho's sake, that they take things easy and they traveled no more than seven or eight miles before stopping at a decent roadside inn, which for once the knight did not mistake for a castle. Indeed,

THEY TRAVELED NO MORE THAN SEVEN OR EIGHT MILES.

since his defeat by the Knight of the White Moon, and the pledge he made to that warrior, his mind did not seem to wander on adventures and romances. Later in the evening he talked to his squire again about finishing with his lashes.

"Well, sir," said Sancho, "it does not matter to me where or when I finish the job. If it's my choice, I'd prefer to finish as soon as possible. I rather favor doing it out among the trees, for they seem to have fellow feeling for me and help me bear up manfully under the suffering."

"I think you ought to take a little time to recover, at least in part, from your severe beating yesterday," answered Don Quixote. "We should put off any more lashes until we get home, which should be the day after tomorrow."

"As your worship pleases," replied Sancho. "I am ready to make an end to the business now, but I will let it wait for a while."

They stayed at the inn that night and most of the next day, taking up their journey again only in the cool of the evening. Very late that night they stopped among some trees to camp and Sancho, seeing the trees were beeches and suited his purpose, persuaded his master that the flogging should be finished there rather than at home. Don Quixote reluctantly consented and Sancho repeated his previous performance.

SANCHO FELL TO HIS KNEES AND SAID,
"OPEN YOUR EYES, BELOVED COUNTRY."

Soon the trees resounded with the strokes of the whip and Sancho howled along with them.

At last his master called to him to stop, for the full count of lashes had been reached, as he reckoned them. Sancho once again borrowed his master's cloak and slept comfortably and peacefully until morning. Don Quixote was cold, but happy in the thought that the spell on the fair Dulcinea was broken at last and he could now hope to see her at any moment in her natural form. After breakfast they set off toward home with light hearts, Don Quixote scanning closely every woman they met along the way to see if she might be the disenchanted Dulcinea coming to thank him.

At last they came to the top of a hill that gave them a view of their native village. Sancho fell to his knees and said: "Open your eyes, beloved country and behold your son Sancho Panza, who has returned to you, not rich, but certainly very flogged. Open your arms and receive your son Don Quixote, who, even if he is defeated by another, is the conqueror of himself—which I have heard is the best of all victories. I return to you with money, despite certain beatings I have had."

"Stop your nonsense," commanded Don Quixote, "and let's hurry home. You can indulge your eloquence there and we can talk about our plans for the future."

Sancho stood up and followed his master into the village. As they entered, they came upon two boys in a dispute and overheard one to say to the other: "You need not trouble yourself about it, for you will never see it again as long as you live."

"Sancho!" exclaimed Don Quixote. "That is an omen to me, signifying that I shall never again see Dulcinea." Sancho was about to answer when a rabbit, trying to escape from hounds that were chasing it, ran between Dapple's legs. Sancho picked it up and handed it to Don Quixote, who immediately saw it as another evil omen, crying out: "The rabbit runs, the hounds chase, and Dulcinea does not appear!"

"You are a strange man, your honor," said Sancho. "Why not suppose that the rabbit represents Dulcinea, who finds safety in your arms from enchanters who are pursuing her? What evil sign is in this?"

Just then the two boys came up to look at the rabbit and Sancho saw that what they had been fighting about was the ownership of a small cage containing some grasshoppers they had collected, and it was to the cage that one of them was referring when he said the other would "never see it again."

Sancho gave the boys two copper pennies for the cage and presented it to Don Quixote, saying, "See how all your evil omens amount to nothing. To me, all such signs have no more to do with what happens than last year's clouds have to do with today's weather. No sensible person should imagine such non-sense. I have heard the priest and you yourself say so. Now let's push on to find our friends and not trouble ourselves with trifles."

They soon came upon the curate and the bachelor Sampson Carrasco, who was no longer masquerading as the Knight of the White Moon. The meeting was friendly on all sides and as they went on together, many people shouted out their welcome to the returned wanderers.

"Here they come! Here's fat Sancho and his donkey turned gray. There's Don Quixote on his old horse, as bony as ever." With such greetings they made their way through the crowd.

News of their arrival spread quickly, and soon Sancho's wife and daughter came running up and embraced him tenderly. But Teresa was struck by the poor appearance of her husband and exclaimed, "How is this? Why do you come back in such a state, on foot and all worn out, not at all like the governor of an island?"

"Silence, Teresa," said Sancho. "Remember, it is always easier to find a hook to hang bacon on than bacon to hang on it. Wait until we get home and then I shall tell you all the news. I dare say at once that I bring back money and that I came by it honestly."

"That's good news anyhow," answered Teresa. "Money is the main thing and whether it comes from here or

DON QUIXOTE DIED PEACEFULLY IN HIS OWN BED,

IN THE MANNER OF A TRUE GENTLEMAN.

there, or how you got it, makes no great difference." With that, mother and daughter escorted Sancho home while Don Quixote and his party went to his house, where he was received affectionately by his niece and the old housekeeper, who set about taking care of him.

But, as time went on, Don Quixote proved to be unmanageable and he could not be persuaded to take a long rest. His glorious career was denied to him for twelve months. He fancied that instead he would become a shepherd for that period and he pestered the curate and the bachelor with such plans, asking them to join him and Sancho in becoming shepherds and poets, as happened often in romances. He said he would find the sheep and the costumes and the flutes and the ribbons and garlands and whatever else shepherds might need, and they would all change their names to make them better suit their new lives. He would call himself Quixotiz and they could be Cusiambo and Carrascon and Sancho would be the shepherd Pancino. He worked out all the details in the most clever and romantic fashion. To keep down his excitement, they pretended to agree to his scheme and promised to join in making it happen once his health was restored.

But nothing would keep him quiet, and his mental unrest brought on a brain fever that kept him laid out in bed for weeks.

The fever gradually passed away, only to leave him in a dying condition. Towards the end his mind got clearer and he became more rational than at any time since he was first affected by the literature of knights-errant he had been reading. He now confessed his madness and asked his friends to forgive him for his many follies and the trouble he had caused them. He made a will and in it he gave his faithful servant Sancho such money as he had on hand, a gift amounting to a small fortune to a man in Sancho's position. To his housekeeper he also left a handsome amount and all the rest of his property he gave to his niece.

His last moments were soothed by the rites of the church, administered by his good friend the curate. And so, after many mad adventures and hazards, Don Quixote died peacefully and naturally in his own house and in his own bed, composed to the last, in the manner of a true gentleman.

Requiescat in Pace

Miguel de Cervantes Saavedra

1547-1616

MIGUEL DE CERVANTES SAAVEDRA WAS BORN IN SPAIN in 1547 to a respected family whose fortunes were sinking. His father was a surgeon (in those days someone who treated wounds and broken bones) who had trouble making ends meet and once was jailed for failing to pay money he owed. The family moved often.

As a boy, Cervantes studied in a grammar school for two years. When he was older he went to college in Seville for one year, but for the most part he educated himself by reading. He loved to go to the theater and when he was grown he wrote more than twenty plays.

As a young man in Madrid, he wounded another man in a duel, possibly fought over an insult to Cervantes' sister. To hide from the law, he ran to southern Spain, where he had relatives. The order for his arrest said that if he was caught

MIGUEL DE CERVANTES SAAVEDRA

his right hand was to be cut off and he was to be banned from Spain for ten years.

But he escaped arrest and was next heard of a year later in Rome, where he became an attendant to the cardinal who served as the Pope's personal valet. The following year, 1570, he enlisted in a Spanish army unit stationed in Italy, probably partly out of zeal to fight the Ottoman Turks, those warlike people of Islamic faith who were threatening to control the Mediterranean Sea and perhaps spread Islam into Christian territories. Cervantes always said the most noble occupation for a man was to be a soldier and he was very proud of his military career.

Trained as a gunner, he fought in the gruesome naval battle of Lepanto, where the Turkish fleet was crushed off the coast of Greece. Cervantes' courage was conspicuous and he was rewarded with letters of favor to the Spanish king. But his left hand was shattered by a bullet and he could not use that arm again. He was also shot in the chest. He healed slowly and rejoined the army in time for the capture of Tunis in 1573.

In 1575, as he sailed home to Spain, his ship was attacked by Algerians. He and his brother Rodrigo were captured and made slaves for the next five years. Cervantes' ransom was set so high, because of the letters to the Spanish king he was carrying, that his family could not afford it. They sold all their

CERVANTES WAS BADLY WOUNDED
IN THE BATTLE OF LEPANTO.

possessions and begged noblemen for more. In the end, Cervantes gave up the money raised for him so that there would be enough for his brother to buy his freedom. Three times Cervantes tried to escape and four times he faced execution by cruel means, but each time he was spared out of the belief that he was worth a high price. He was a hero among the slaves for his coolness, wisdom, and his strong sense of honor. He always was ready to risk his life for a chance to be free.

He was on a ship, waiting to be taken to Constantinople by his owner, the Turkish governor of Algiers, when his ransom was paid by a priest. After twelve years absence, he went home, deeply in debt for his freedom. He hoped for employment from King Philip II, who did send him back to Algiers on a secret mission, but after that he got nothing.

So he turned to writing. In 1584 he published a romance, *La Galatea*, which was just the sort of fanciful romance that he made fun of in *Don Quixote*.

That same year he married Catalina de Palacios, who was eighteen years younger than he, and who had a modest income from her family's small property. Three years later Cervantes was appointed as the king's commissary (someone who gathers supplies for the army or navy) in La Mancha. He traveled the region seizing wheat and olive oil to supply the Armada being built to invade England. But commissaries were disliked and the job caused him trouble. The bishop of Seville excommunicated Cervantes (forbade him to receive the sacraments of the Catholic Church) for taking wheat from a monastery.

Cervantes twice tried to get posts with the Spanish colonial government in America, where he believed he could make a fortune, but was refused. At last he was made a tax collector, but he lost some money he had taken in and was jailed in Seville for several months because of the shortage. There, at age 50, he began writing *Don Quixote,* the greatest work in all Spanish literature.

Part I of the novel appeared seven years later, in 1605, and was an immediate and huge success. It was especially admired in England and France. Cervantes had sold the rights to his book before it was printed, however, and he did not profit from its sales. An unknown author published what he claimed was the rest of *Don Quixote,* which so upset Cervantes that he completed Part II in 1615.

Cervantes died at home one year later, probably from the effects of diabetes. He was buried in a nearby convent in an unmarked grave.